A Taste of Midnight

A Taste of Midnight
Sensual Vampire Stories

edited by Cecilia Tan

Circlet Press, Inc.
Cambridge, MA

A Taste of Midnight

Printed in Canada
ISBN 1-885865-23-6

First Edition October 2000

Circlet Press is distributed in the USA and Canada by the LPC Group. Circlet Press is distributed in the UK and Europe by Turnaround Ltd. Circlet Press is distributed in Australia by Bulldog Books.

For a catalog, information about our other imprints, review copies, and other information, please write to:

Circlet Press, Inc.
1770 Massachusetts Avenue #278
Cambridge, MA 02140
circlet-info@circlet.com
http://www.circlet.com

Contents

A Taste of Midnight

Introduction

The vampire is a wily, secretive creature—we think we know them so well, and yet, is it not the unknown that attracts us, as well? The vampire is the perfect erotic conundrum; we want mortal danger and immortality, seduction and surrender, ecstasy and darkness, pleasure and pain.

We are attracted to what is enduring about the vampire myth, but at the same time, we want something new, something different, something that can still startle and surprise us. And herein lies the challenge for the intrepid vampire writer or anthologist—how to give you what you need to satisfy your hunger, and yet not tire you with the same old buffet of capes and fangs and bloodsucking.

So you won't find anyone in a red satin lined cape nibbling the neck of any virgin in this book. What you will find are goddesses with secrets, the pleasure to be found at the edge of danger, and vampires with some needs of their own. In some of these tales, vampires are hunted and persecuted, some are mavens of ritual magic, others add new meaning to the word "night life."

And there is more to come, as it would seem that the appeal of the erotic vampire is as eternal as the vampire itself is purported to be. This is the fourth volume in Circlet Press's erotic vampire series, and we are already at work on a fifth (entitled *Blood Surrender*). We will be bringing Amarantha Knight's erotic retellings of *Dracula*, *Carmilla*, and other horror classics back into print in coming seasons, as well. Because you, dear reader, have an appetite which is as insatiable as the vampire's.

Drink deep, and enjoy.

Cecilia Tan
Cambridge, MA

Descend

Pagan O'Leary

"Ashes and blood here, pleasure and pain." The hiss of the hawker stops you, louder than that pulse in your head. Dead eyes look out from the deep hood and a bony finger beckons. Shiver before the gatekeeper, look past. Skulls should not smile that way. But nearer, yes, move in so close you feel the chill seep into your bones. Nearer, nearer oh god to that door. Pay your obols to Charon and enter.

Heat and red lights. The silence laces numbing tendrils around your brain, sucking you into it. Descend. One step, slowly, and another. Descend. Long coat whisks around your ankles as you stalk this tainted realm.

Mistress Dani in too-shiny black vinyl. "On your knees and beg to serve me, lout." Voice sharper than whipcracks, you like that, and her whip snaps the air, bites the rock below her feet. See the sparks and think of fire swirling, a lush golden gown of heat surging with a hundred red tongues to lick at her body. Clothe her in gold fire and whisper, "Dance for me, my beauty."

Not here, not now. Shake your head and pass, let her wonder. Descend.

The green room, yes, sickly light and twisted forms writhing. The taste of anguish sweet on your lips. Such sounds to haunt the soul, cast your arms wide and let that music embrace you. Dark they move, masked demons applying their torments with icy precision. Your proxy. They delight you. But later—not yet.

Who set these stones along the walls? Black, sharp, razor edge upon your fingertips and you taste the blood with a graceful lash of your tongue. Soothing and warm copper wet flows to that pulse in your head. Thrumming. Driving. Descend.

A sibilant whisper calls you forward; you stumble and grasp the bars with clammy hands. Press your face to the cold iron, eyes closed, mold yourself to the cage. Wait. Don't look. It will be too glorious, hold back from that moment, and yet you hear them sigh, they moan, they breathe. With fright, ah, then they've seen you, your silhouette looming. Rustles of movement, but no they can't run. They wait, wait for you. Open . . . see them, shrinking within themselves, screaming eyes. And choose.

Now to your room and you pace it impatient. Let it begin. Let them bring her and chain her and leave her to your mercies. Fragile in her chains. Soft, warm skin. You touch it delicately but she cringes. Smile in triumph, for her fear permits you everything. Fear feeds the pounding, the pulse in your head, inflames the yearning to devour and consume. Slow. Throb. Closer, the stroking to waken her heat.

Ah, to feed now at this moment, to crush her beneath you and drown in the dark tide. If you dared. But she would slip from your grasp at that last glorious moment and slide out of reach, gone, free. You would never descend these stairs again. No, she must be ready.

Strum on that fear as you cherish her flesh and lure her past thought, past reason. It's for this that she sells herself, this ride past the edge to her shadow place of floating, the place where she changes. Balance her there between wanting and dread, make her beg, make her kneel. Then she's ready.

Oh the pulse rocks your body, grip the handle of the whip and growl to the shadows that you will feed, you will feast. Croon softly for that first strip of red, the thrill of it. "Sing for me," a coaxing request, yes, you will conduct her cries with the swing of your arm. Lean into it, feel it, as her screaming flesh lures you closer. Become the pulse and throb into her head, her darkness, beating, falling, leaving. Make her scream, make her bleed, make her fly.

Beneath you she melts and is lost to the world. Capture the rhythm, ride it. It's flowing, molten in her veins, changing her to a creature of impulse and urge and instinct who can feed you, sate you, and then feed you again.

She calls you with her voiceless writhing and you press against her, wet and burning, taste her and relish the sweet hints. She pulls you with her, deeper, darker. Heavy air holds you poised on the cliff edge of falling then she yields. Ravenous, brutal, swallowing you inside her until the scream, beyond the rest, and her head falls back in surrender.

The one timeless moment that brought you below. Tremble. Cherish it. And with grace you now feed.

Goddess of the Wine
Kate Hill

"Goddess, forgive me."
  Beauty.
  "I have sinned."
  Pure.
  "Though they didn't believe me."
  Red.
  The beauty of the Goddess with her pure red lips.
  He had been chosen, but already had failed.
  She lived by the shadow, he by the light, yet once each year they would intertwine and glimpse their separate worlds. Through that intimate exchange she could face the light and he could envelop the darkness, but only if the ritual was performed, unchanged.
  He should never have spoken of it aloud, even in private, but he had. His brothers had overheard him and laughed, not

believing that he, the youngest and least handsome of them all, had been chosen by the Goddess.

He knelt by the altar, the sand hot upon his knees, even through the white ritual robe he wore. Closing his eyes, he inhaled deeply of the incense mixed from the herbs and flowers he'd gathered, dried, and crushed, as the ritual ordered. Narcissus and orange blossom dominated his every breath when she'd appeared to him in the dreams.

Always cloaked in white, with delicate hands light as desert sand, she reached out to him, though they never touched. Still, the sound of her voice, the graceful movements of her fingers, left him breathless with anticipation of the coming ritual. He awoke swollen with longing only to force his rebellious body into submission.

Three days after their first communication, he had traveled into the desert until he'd reached the altar which had stood, carved into the shape of the Goddess, since the beginning.

Tonight at dusk she would meet him and consummate the ritual. At least he hoped so. Pride had coaxed him to speak aloud of the forbidden; now it was within her right to refuse him that which he most desired.

His blue eyes squinted against the sun. She'd told him how brilliant she'd heard it was. It would be her first time as well as his. She was the youngest of her kind, which was why she had chosen him. Though they had spoken only twice in dreams, she said she'd already felt bonded to him.

How would she feel when she realized what he'd done? Perhaps she knew and would deny him, not even meet him. What if he had truly sacrificed her convergence with the light, ruining his joining with the darkness. He'd listened to the ones who had already participated in the ritual, and had seen the result of the power they had felt, but it wasn't enough. He wanted to feel it. Would he?

"Goddess, forgive me," he whispered as the sun set, cooling the desert heat.

Endless swells of sand tinted red by the setting sun surrounded him. He waited, motionless, until the incense burned out. Still he was alone.

She would not come.

Wind stirred his hair, caressed his cheek, but the wind should not speak—

"Will you join the darkness to guide me to the light?"

He turned, heartbeat quickening, and gazed upon her. The Goddess.

Tall and lithe she stood before him, wearing only a silver necklace fashioned into the shape of a snake about the delicate column of her throat, its eyes two rubies as large and dominant as the flushed peaks of her nipples which tipped her breasts, pale as the hovering moon. Dark hair hung straight and gleaming down her back, brushing her rounded buttocks. Her eyes were a mossy green in the dimness.

"I thought you wouldn't come," he whispered. "I spoke of our forbidden—"

"It took time, but I convinced the others to let me come to you. We are so much alike. I know that you are the only one who can truly please me, and I know that I can pleasure you as well. Tonight we will become each other then you will join your brothers in the sacrifice of blood. All we ask is one chalice filled with your sacred wine. Just one chalice each month on which we survive."

"I will give you whatever you want." He stepped forward, his hands clenched into fists to keep from touching her. How he wanted to devour her unearthly loveliness with so much more than his eyes.

"But first, I will give to you."

She stepped up to him, her voluptuous mouth drawing on his while her cool hands slid the robe from his body, caressing the hard muscles of his youthful arms and chest. Her nails, long and painted burgundy, raked his abdomen until he flinched beneath the sensual tickling motion. He closed his eyes as her mouth moved from his to trail down his neck, pausing at the pounding pulse at the base of his throat before continuing downward.

Her hands came to rest on his side so that she could feel his heart beating against her palm. She could hear the rush of blood within his veins, could taste the saltiness of his skin beneath her tongue as she resumed her sensual journey down his body, licking his navel with slow, moist strokes.

The ritual had been born when the first vampire made love to a mortal without taking his life. It was learned that through a sharing of such benign passion, both could temporarily enjoy the benefits of their separate natures.

The bond forged between a vampire and a mortal who shared such an experience was unyielding. Since then, vampires and mortals lived apart, except for the ritual meetings. Mortals sacrificed a portion of their blood in exchange for the chance to bond with a vampire and create a union deeper than marriage, deeper than love.

"Touch me." the Goddess spoke, awakening him from the sensual state, guiding his hands to the smoothness of her breasts.

He stared at his own hands, which held the ivory mounds soon to be flushed pink with his own passion and blood. His thumbs moved in a circular motion over the erect nipples, causing her to draw a sharp breath and arch her neck, her full lips falling open slightly, revealing the fine, gleaming points of her canines. Rather than being frightened, he found them to be particularly erotic, and wondered what he would feel when they broke his skin.

"Not yet," she whispered. "You're not ready for that."

He looked surprised, and she explained that the mental link which had drawn them together still bound them, and that it would add to the fervor of their union.

"You're so beautiful, I'm almost afraid to touch you," he murmured against her lips, "You're like no woman I've ever known."

"Some pleasures we share with mortals." She gasped as his fingers again found her nipples. Understanding swept over him with the first of her shudders. He pulled her into his arms and lay her on the altar, the vaguest hint of incense still in the air.

"Now you understand me," she murmured in abandon as he caressed her with his hands, his lips drawing upon one hardened nipple until she cried out with pleasure. Her breathing quickened, as with a mortal woman, dragging his along with it. His mouth moved from her breast so that his tongue could leave a hot, wet trail down her belly. His hands kneaded her inner thighs, moving higher until his thumbs brushed the wetness between her legs, and stroked the patch of hair, glossy and black as upon her head.

His shaft was hard, erect, the velvet skin a throbbing veil of sensation which longed for the heated enclosure of her flesh.

He eased himself over her, their panting breaths mingling, limbs intertwined. Her nipples scraped his sleek, hairless chest. She caressed his nape, entangled her fingers in the thickness of his wheat-colored hair.

She closed her eyes, only wanting to hear and to feel. His heart beat an allegro rhythm; his entire body throbbed against hers, enveloping her in his mortal pleasure until she knew she must take from him or die of desire. She licked his throat, her tongue resting upon the protruding vein on the side of his neck. With her senses heightened, she felt as if his blood was ready to burst through the skin without aid from her needle-sharp fangs.

He was close to his moment of crisis. She had to time it perfectly, or else the ritual would fail.

He pumped steadily into her body, his back slick with sweat beneath her hands, his body trembling with a keener pleasure than he thought possible. In his passion, he momentarily forgot he was making love to the Goddess, but simply sought release from the sensual agony building within him. Then he felt the slightest twinge of pain as her teeth pierced his skin as deeply as he had pierced her body. He cried out at the sudden shock and flood of sexual stimulation so great that he whirled down into blackness as waves of orgasm flooded him, incredible for any mortal man.

At the first taste of his blood, the Goddess reached her own climax, her body shuddering as the sweet, red liquid melted into her, heating her, flushing pink her pale skin. She held his spent and trembling body close as she fed, feeling the harsh rasp of his breath against her, loving the heat of his perspiring skin and the hardness of his chest against her soft breasts and still-peaked nipples.

Too soon she forced herself to stop drinking, not wanting to kill him and destroy the beauty of what they had just shared. She licked the last drops of blood from his skin, then closed her eyes, still buried beneath him, until he stirred slightly. Before he fully awakened, she shifted her weight, and with one red-tipped finger, made an incision on top of her right breast. Warm blood beaded against her skin, and she guided his mouth to her breast so that he could drink of what he'd given her.

Slowly at first, he suckled on her, his tongue drawing the sweetness of her blood into him. Instantly he was aroused, in spite of the intensity of his last orgasm. He pierced her entrance, still flowing from their earlier joining, and challenged her with long, fast strokes. She encouraged him with hoarse cries of lust, her nails raking his biceps, her neck arched back, catching the moonlight. He tore his mouth from her breast only to shriek with uncontrollable pleasure as his climax drew him from reality into her world of immortal passion. He fell upon her, his bloody lips resting upon her throat, dampening the white skin. When he finally caught his breath, he spoke with reverence.

"That was—" he began, then paused as his eyes opened and he saw the night as he never imagined it could be.

He stood up, his naked body pale in the moonlight, and looked across the desert, seeing every night creature, every white grain of sand glistening like diamond dust in the brightness of the moon.

"This is what you see." He turned to her, his eyes wide as they witnessed a night brighter and more beautiful than the day could ever be. "No wonder you can't bear the sunlight."

"But at dawn I will." She smiled slightly, her lips stained as red as the snake's ruby eyes. "Tomorrow I will know what you see by day, as you now know what I see by night. We are forever bonded."

"Forever bonded." He knelt by the altar, taking her hands in his. "Goddess, I love you."

"And I love you."

"Even though I spoke the forbidden and nearly destroyed the ritual?"

"Yes. I loved you since our first communication. I knew I had to have you, if only just once."

His entire being rebelled against such a torturous restriction.

"Only once? But we will love each other again?"

"No." Tears shone in her green eyes. "Not us. That is my punishment for meeting you, though you disturbed the ancient ritual. Never again will I see the sun, nor will you truly see the night."

"There's got to be a way. . . ."

She shook her head, her dark hair concealing her anguished face. "Should we continue to meet yearly as other couples do, our mental bond will become so strong that you will know where I am and what I feel at all times. You will know where my kind rest. The others fear that you cannot be trusted and will divulge our whereabouts the same way you spoke aloud of our meeting. They worry that if you do, the few ignorant mortals who spurn our existence will use your knowledge to destroy us."

For a moment he was unable to draw a breath. He would never harm her or her kind, especially now that they had coupled and his love for her was as deep and true as the night.

"We have to convince them that I'd never betray you."

"I've tried. The old ones will not bend, at least not soon."

"Then there is a chance?" The eagerness in his eyes was painful for her, with her perception of the Elders, to behold, but she cared for him too much to leave him without hope.

"Perhaps someday they will consider allowing us to bond again."

In spite of her effort to console him, their union had already enabled him to feel more of her emotions than either of them realized. He sensed her lie.

"What have I done?" He drew her into his arms, felt her tears dampen his chest as his own fell on her night-dark hair. His infantile bragging had brought punishment upon them both. "Why didn't you pick someone else, someone you could share a lifetime with?"

"Because," she looked up at him, her hand caressing his cheek. "One drink of your wine will sustain me better than a thousand sips from one I do not love."

"I may never see you again."

"You have only to think of me, and I will be there."

"But not in the flesh."

"In your mind, and in your heart, for always."

"And for now?"

"We have until the sun rises. Then I must go."

"I will love you until then."

"This is your one night to see with my eyes. Surely you don't want to waste it."

"All I want is you."

Her eyes moistened, softened, so that they appeared almost mortal, and she went willingly into his embrace.

"There is an oasis, not far from here," she said. "We sometimes sleep there when dawn comes too soon and we've been out too long. Come there with me now."

Dropped in the desert like an emerald in miles of ivory silk, the oasis gave them refuge from the stern indifference of the ritual altar. Tall palms shaded them from the moon, cooling them in shadow, as he lay on his back and she stretched out beside him, her head resting on his shoulder.

"Legend has it that the first vampire and mortal ever to perform the ritual did so here," she said, her fingertips drawing random circles on his chest, the pad of her index finger brushing one of his nipples.

"I wonder if he felt as I do. Everything seems so much more beautiful than before. I can even see the birds nesting in the top of that tree."

She tossed him a bewitching smile as she held up a single perfect feather which had fallen from the nest to the ground beside them.

His eyes followed the feather's trail as she waved it across his abdomen, scarcely touching his skin. She brushed it along the length of his organ, and watched as it hardened from her carnal implication.

The feather moved across his thighs, traced the creases where his legs joined his hips.

"You are a wanton tease." He sighed against her lips as she moved to kiss him.

"Seduction is the vampire's most practiced art," she replied, sliding her tongue between his lips, stroking the slippery softness of his inner cheek.

His arms slid about her, pulling her on top of him. One of her legs fell between his, so that his hardness pressed against her hip. His hands splayed across her slim, supple back.

Their tongues fenced, moist and desperate lovers, until even the vampire was breathless with her lust. She pushed away from him only to kneel between his feet. She lowered her lips to his ankle and licked and kissed every inch of skin on his leg, loving the texture of the rough, curling hair, until she reached his inflamed organ. The heady aroma of his lust filled her vampiric senses. She took him in her mouth, her tongue lapping the ruby crown of his erection until he gasped aloud, begging her not to stop. His fingers tightened in her dark hair, though through a haze of desire he made a conscious effort not to hurt her. She seemed to know his own body better than he did as she kept him on the verge of orgasm, not allowing him to reach that delightful zenith until she was ready. Her sultry lips drew one last time upon his shaft, lingering on the flushed head before dropping a nibbling kiss upon it.

He stared at her through half-closed eyes, his heart pounding, his body longing for that final surrender.

Smiling flirtatiously, she stretched out on the ground, her arms reaching above her head, giving lift to her rounded breasts. An animalistic sound erupted from his throat as he loomed over her, licking her breasts as she had done to his legs, leaving not the slightest bit of skin untouched. He found a sensitive place beneath her breast and licked it relentlessly, causing her to jerk with ticklish pleasure. He took a nipple in his mouth and sucked forcefully while gently nipping.

His mouth moved down her body, followed by his softly caressing hands. He dipped his head between her legs, steadying her by the hips, and licked her engorged vulva while listening intently to her moans of pleasure. Her womanly scent mingled with the aroma of narcissus and orange blossom, reminding him of the incense he'd burned at the ritual altar. His tongue penetrated her entrance, drawing on her sensual elixir as if it could nourish him as his blood nourished her.

He paused for a moment to glance at her face. Her eyes were closed, dark lashes trembling against niveous skin. There was a faint blush in her cheeks that would have been imperceptible to his human eyes, had he not drank of her unworldly blood. Her sultry, kiss-swollen lips were parted as she drew sips of air, her teeth sharp and pearly in the moonlight.

She cried out in abandon as he slid up her body and entered her swiftly, pushing them both over the brink of control. Her legs locked about his waist, forcing him even deeper within her, so that her flesh clung to his like a trembling velvet glove.

For what seemed like hours they rested in each other's arms, staring up at the moon and stars through the trees swaying faintly in the temperate wind.

"How can I ever be happy knowing I'll never hold you again?" he murmured against her hair. "What will I say to you when we must part?"

"Say nothing," she told him. "No words will describe what we've felt this night, or what I feel for you, or you for me. Only know that we have loved, and will always love each other."

"Always," he whispered, kissing her cardinal lips, memorizing the curve of her cheek, the pigment of her skin as he saw it with his preternatural eyes. Within hours he would only have memories of his vampire senses and of the Goddess who gave them to him.

He held her until the dawn when she smiled at him and wept upon seeing the sun as he had upon seeing the night. He watched her walk naked across the desert sands, back to her own kind.

"Goddess, forgive me," he whispered, tears overflowing his all-too-human eyes as he remembered the piquant beauty of her pure red lips.

She disappeared into the rippling waves of desert heat, and he walked from the oasis without looking back.

Waiting for Sunset
Elizabeth Thorne

Night fell earlier each night in Chicago, and waiting for sunset became easier every day. It was hard to sit a chemistry lab idly exploring the nature of organic solvents when the undead were waking to prowl, but at least it killed the time. Besides, I liked the way the instructor was staring at my legs. He looked so guilty, but it didn't stop him from looking back. When I pulled my cross from between my breasts and stroked it absentmindedly while calculating the next reaction mixture he actually managed to turn a little green. I had always thought that was a figure of speech. I made a mental note that once again biology was stranger then fiction, and congratulated myself for having proven once again that there is nothing quite so reliable as good old Catholic guilt.

So I had a tendency toward predatory. It wasn't my fault that even on a good day I had trouble convincing anyone that

27

I was over sixteen. . . . It certainly wasn't my choice. People
were always afraid to take advantage of me. I suppose it was
out of some misguided concern that I was going to run
home and call for daddy, but it drove me crazy. I looked so
respectable that I could have painted the word *bait* on my
forehead without the hungry ones even batting an eye. I'd
actually tried it once, a few years earlier, when I had gone
to one of the more notorious leather bars. I was rewarded
for my efforts by no fewer then three beautiful women pat-
ting me on the head and calling me cute. I've always hated
that. What made it even worse was that one of them was a
vampire. That was back when people tolerated the undead
out of fear. The authorities couldn't find them during the
day, and couldn't hunt them effectively at night, so they let
the carnivores be. Some even found a niche among people
who appreciated their way of feeding, or wanted to offer a
bit more variety in the preparation of their diet. Now
though, technology has left no room for legends.

Ever since DNA cards superseded other forms of identifi-
cation and hard currency, vampires have been on their way
to becoming an endangered species. What churches failed
to eradicate for thousands of years, bureaucracy may
accomplish in a few decades. It's hard to offer a bloodprint
to a merchant that matches your recorded identity when
the DNA in your blood changes every time you feed, and
without a card there's no housing, transportation, or access
to public spaces. Heat scanning makes it challenging for
even the undead to hide from notice for long. The government justifies the random neighborhood sweeps by saying
that they're the only way that everyone can be taken care
of and kept safe. Not much has changed for most people
since the old days—and they say they like the feeling of
security—but I've never known how they can't realize that

they're falling into a trap. With all the monitoring, it requires a great deal of creativity to be anything other than mainstream if you don't want it to catch up with you later. Maybe the silent majority likes that. I know they enjoy the fact that they are driving off the predators, but their lack of foresight makes me sick.

The sun was setting, so I figured it was time to prowl. At least getting ready was easy. When you're going hunting, it's not so much a matter of what you put on, as what you take off. The cross, of course, was hung on the doorknob so that I wouldn't forget to wear it to classes, and the rest of my "good girl drag" I put neatly into my closet. After taking a quick shower to get rid of any traces of the morning's perfume, I slipped into a ragged pink dress and my biker jacket, combed my hair, and tried vainly not to look like a kid playing dress-up in her sister's clothes.

Things being as they were, I had been rather surprised to see the newspaper reports of the murders down in Boystown. The fact that the corpses were a bit short on blood was buried in the last paragraph of the articles. Denial. I figured that having thought that the vampires were all gone from our part of the world made it difficult for the press to admit that we hadn't exorcized our demons once and for all. I couldn't have been the only person happy that our legends still walked the earth, but I was probably one of the least surprised to see the proof in print. There was a woman I had noticed haunting the bars who was hard to look at in a way that made me weak in the knees. All that beautiful black hair and pale skin: If you noticed her at all she fit right in with the Goth contingent. Except that most people didn't notice her, and the first time I had seen the way their eyes skimmed right over her, my pulse began to race for the first time in almost a year. I'd been trying to catch her eye ever since, but I knew I looked like too much trouble to be good prey. Most of her victims had been lost boy types—nowadays not nameless, but also not likely to be missed. There hadn't been a story for almost a week, so I decided that it was finally the time to be not just quarry, but temptation.

When I got off the el I saw her standing at the corner of Belmont and Clark talking to one of the punk kids outside the donut store. Certain that the boy she was talking to had no idea of the trouble I was trying to save him from, I followed them as they walked around the corner to a darkened bar. It was smoky and after I stopped at the bar for a whisky (which was going to show on my card if anyone bothered to look, but the alcohol was a good disinfectant), I waited until she sat. I tried not to take the time to think about how bad an idea my whole plan was, and instead took comfort in the fact that being cocky and fearless had served me well so far in life. No reason for that to change. I hoped. With a great deal of luck, and due to no small amount of practice, I managed to trip over the edge of her chair and land on the glass which I had thrown down hard enough to shatter at the start of my fall. I said a small prayer in thanks to the manager of all bars who were cheap about their stemware.

Oh no. My arm is bleeding. I'm so upset. I felt more then a little guilty about being that conniving, but if she didn't think all this was her idea, she wouldn't get me where she wanted me. Planning this had taken too much effort to be foiled by subtlety, so I brushed my hair out of my face and, Oops! there was a smear of blood at the base of my throat. She reached down to help me stand, and I started to offer her the hand that was covered in blood. As I pretended to realize my error and began to slowly draw it back, she grabbed it and pulled me to my feet.

"Can I help you get somewhere?" she asked in a voice which under the concerned tone was still sultry enough to melt the polar ice caps.

"No. I mean no one is expecting me. I guess I should go somewhere to clean this up, but. . . ."

Game, set, and match. She practically carried me out the door.

She had made some noise about going back to her place where there was antiseptic, and when we got outside and started walking, I made my move. We were going past one of those nice dark alleyways—the sort that leads to the back entrance of some anonymous bar—when I stumbled against her, and whispering in her ear told her that I knew what she was. Standing up straight, I looked her in the eyes and said, "I hope you're hungry. I've been waiting for you for a long time." I couldn't help but grin at the expression of shock on her face. I think she was actually a little nervous until, keeping her eyes locked with mine, I backed farther into the alley, slipped out a piece of my broken glass and drew it slowly in a line across the top of my breast. She didn't come closer as the blood started to fall, so I dropped the humor and continued speaking, "I can keep cutting, opening myself for you, but if you want . . . well . . . I can make myself bleed, but I need you to make me scream."

I heard a moan, and suddenly I was no longer in control. She threw me back against the wall, one arm pinning my wrists above my head, the other pressing against my stomach as I felt her tongue begin to collect the drops of blood that had started to stain the front of my dress. Then her mouth began to move, and all of a sudden the dress wasn't there anymore. I could feel her breath as she moved over my skin, and I was beginning to sigh at the feeling of her tongue on my breast when her canines sunk an inch deep into the flesh behind my nipple. I could feel her sucking inside my skin as I began to scream. Her hand came away from my waist, and she raised her beautiful blood covered face to mine and said, "You asked for this. You wanted this." before raking her nails across my neck and shoulder and leaning back down to create a new set of holes only millimeters away from the first. Her free hand continued its descent and now those knife sharp nails were playing with my other breast scratching, twisting, and pulling, until I was moaning with the pleasure as well as the pain. The suction increased inside my chest where she continued to feed, and I heard myself shamelessly begging for more. She must have heard me because the pulling sensation stopped, and I heard a whisper in my ear.

"Little one, you really did know what you wanted. It would be a shame to let a pretty girl like you go to waste when I could have you again and again. You're such a precious find. My family would be jealous of this pleasure."

"Please don't stop. I'll come to you again, whenever you wish. You can even kill me as long as you promise not to stop."

"Patience. You make me so happy, why shouldn't I share?"

And then, before I could understand, she was kissing me. Except I felt her teeth in my lip and was dazed at the taste of the metallic tang of my own blood. The shock of the contact was almost enough to make me stop missing the pain, but then she lifted me higher and her hand, those nails, were between my legs. First three, then four fingers found their way inside of me, her thumb wrapping around me to press against my clit, and I was no longer hanging from my wrists and her mouth as she let some of my weight fall onto her hand. The feeling of penetration was amazing as she stroked inside me gently and used her hand to raise me upward to sit on a nearby dumpster. She sucked the drying blood from my breasts, drew back to look me in the eye and the gentleness was over as she slowly pulled her fingers out of my body, inch by inch clawing bloody furrows through my inner walls. Keeping her hand pressed tightly against me, she licked at the blood that was pooling in her palm, and her fingers pushed their way back inside. Over and over again, and then I felt the knife sharp point of her thumb press menacingly against the base of my clit, and I was coming violently, spasming blood. As she sucked the life from inside me, I thought the pleasure would never end.

I must have passed out from the loss of blood, because I woke up the next afternoon in my own bed. I remembered vaguely that she had found the DNA card in my jacket and used it to get me back in, because in a brief moment of consciousness, still giddy from the endorphins, I'd caught my self thinking that metal must not conduct religion or the cross on the doorknob would be forcing her to leave me out in the cold. I had slept most of the morning, so I felt okay to go to class, but I'd gotten dressed and put on my cross before I realized what the memory might mean. Sure enough, when I checked, the card was nowhere to be found. Unless I reported it, until the next time she got hungry she was going to be passing as me. If I reported it they might wonder why I was still alive, but if I didn't I couldn't leave my secured building or get any food. Worse, if I told, the first time she used the card they'd catch her and kill her; unlike the other endangered predators, vampires aren't among the protected species. So it was let her be killed, and be forced to go through some church-sponsored cleansing ritual, or stay locked in my room with my life subject to her whim. I couldn't help thinking that it might not be so bad.

After all, if she wanted to keep the card stocked at its current levels, she'd have to let me continue going to class, and my room could be an excellent place for her to hide during the day. Even at a Catholic college, who would notice an extra sleeping body in a girls' dormitory? I hoped my plan was along the lines of what she had in mind. Waiting for sunset could become almost pleasant if I had someone to wait for.

She came back. Which was good because I didn't think I could have sent the message that would have had her killed, and yet I also knew that I wasn't ready to die. My post-bloodshed bliss had passed not long after it arrived, and I'd begun to worry. When you've spent most of your life wanting something and then you drop into her lap, the number of ways things can go wrong increases sharply in magnitude. I had changed into my fuzzy robe and optimistically spent the afternoon doing homework for the aforementioned annoyance of an organic lab—knowing that if lived long enough I needed a passing grade. Having fallen asleep around the time I normally would have headed to dinner, I woke when I found myself gasping for air with a hand around my throat. A vampire's hand. Attached to the angry vampire who was kneeling above me holding my diary. It's at times like that when I wish that more of the legends were true. Especially the ones that claim that a vampire can't enter your dwelling without being invited in. It hadn't seemed to me that begging someone to be their next meal could be considered implied consent, but what did I know? From a spiritual viewpoint, one lives inside one's body, so it could be argued that I had done the masochist's equivalent of asking her in for a drink. But that was no reason to read my diary. At least, I assumed that was why she was mad. No one hates to be manipulated quite so much as a manipulator. I started to wonder if most people's thoughts were this sarcastic when they were being choked, and it occurred to me that it was probably time for me to attempt making the switch to practical. I'd try humor, if it didn't make her let go, at least it would probably goad her into killing me quickly.

"Statistics show that most people are killed by a friend, or a member of the family." I croaked out, "and us not even properly introduced. Who ever said that statistics don't lie?" For a brief moment the anger flashed brighter across her face, but then she laughed. "Although some might say that it's been the equivalent of a formal introduction." I shuddered when I realized what I'd said. The rush of oxygen must have been making me giddy.

"I should kill you for what you presumed," she snarled, the anger coming back briefly to haunt her eyes. I could see by the tension in her lips the effort it was taking for her to control it. "But in the long run doing so might just kill *me*. You were right when you said that it's hard for a vampire to live in the world the way it is today. I almost got caught in a sweep a few days ago, but they didn't find my body until after the sun had set. I need an identity. What you proposed is a way for me to have one. From midnight until dawn, I will be you, or from now until forever, you will be dead. My name is Gillian, and you will consider yourself mine."

I should kill you for what you presumed. I have always lacked respect for melodrama, and although admittedly it wasn't the easiest time to be matter-of-fact, at least she could have avoided being predictable. Irritation gave me enough strength to push her off me, and I sat up. "You had no cause to invade my privacy. I gave you my body freely, but reading my diary. . . . Obviously age doesn't teach you manners." I shook my head, and turned away to stare at the paintings on the wall, "What can I say? Because of your presumption, you know that what you ask is all I have ever wanted. So I accept. I bartered you the right to kill me last night, and I will not break my word. You can share my life until such time as you choose to end it. My name, as you know, is Rose."

"Well, Rose." She walked around to stand in front of me. "Your petals are drooping. I think I'll have a little snack, and then you should go to sleep for the night. You can refresh yourself in the morning. When I come in, I'll take the bed."

Rose. Your petals are drooping. For gods' sake, did she actually think I hadn't heard all the stupid flower jokes a thousand times before? And *she'd* take the bed? I could have cursed the person who designed the cell block which was masquerading as my dormitory. Why should a girl get stuck with a windowless room just because she wanted a little privacy?

I felt her hand twining itself into my hair.

A snack. Oh. *Oh.*

She pulled my head back and looked into my eyes. "Rose, I really am glad to have found you. No one has wanted me like this in a very long time."

Her hand slowly tilted me back farther and I felt her breath at the base of my throat. Her fangs penetrated slowly, almost gently, as she stroked my back, and I wrapped my arms around her waist to press her close. I wanted to show her that I was there freely. She should know that I was hers freely.

Her skin beneath her clothing was cool and smooth, like living silk, and as she began to draw out my blood I could almost feel her start to warm. I touched her throat with my fingers and could feel my heartbeat in her veins. One blood, two bodies. It made me feel more than human. Holding her close, nursing her like a child, I fell asleep in her arms.

Pale Smoke

Raven Kaldera

"When you walk through a cloud of smoke," Feather whispered in my ear, "what does your body feel like to it? Do you feel like a lover? Like a violator? Does it caress you with desperate need, longing for you to notice, to respond to its love and desire?" She took a drag on her slender gilt pipe and exhaled a breath of felissium smoke my way.

I decided not to breathe for the moment. Not that the smoke would make me high, anyway, but I was beginning to hate its sickly sweetish smell. I turned my head away, though, for Feather's benefit. She stroked my hair where it tumbled over my shoulders, and laughed at me, lazily. Like a cat who knows the mouse isn't going anywhere.

"Look at me, darling," she murmured. I didn't respond. I hated playing her games, knowing I could never win except by outlasting her, outwaiting her. My reticence annoyed

her, as I knew it would. "Look at me, Tonio," she com-
manded, yanking me back by a fistful of my hair. I fell into
the pillows and my gaze caught hers unwillingly. She stared
at me until my eyes unfocused; I wondered if she was trying to hypnotize me.

Then she took another drag on her pipe and lowered her
lips to mine, glistening scarlet and irresistible. I let her kiss
me without thinking—one could go into trance while kissing Feather—and then realized my error when she breathed
the whole cloud of felissium smoke into my lungs. I pushed
her aside, coughing and expelling it, and she laughed at me
again, like the tinkle of bells on a wind chime. "So sensitive," she murmured, "to such a little thing."

"Don't do that," I said, not expecting she'd do anything
but laugh again, and I was right. Then she was on me, biting playfully at my chest, my ear, my throat, sucking on the
flesh. I didn't worry that she'd be able to bite through it;
she'd tried before, and failed. Besides, I knew she wanted
me to give her immortality willingly, to offer it on my
knees. *In her dreams*, I thought to myself, and sighed.

Feather came up off me, annoyed again. "Ungrateful bas-
tard," she said, and bounced up out of bed, black silk
peignoir slipping over my thighs like a whisper of spite. She
grabbed a hairbrush and began to give her black hair the
hundred-stroke treatment, something she only did when
angry. One shoulder of the peignoir had slipped down,
revealing her white flesh. I stared at the back of her pale
neck and counted to twenty, then repeated the entire
Zavaret meditation mantra, word for word, six times. It
wasn't helping much.

Black hair, smooth and glossy like a river to the small of
her back—she was so proud of it—and skin like old ivory,
long tilted dark eyes. Feather never wore perfume any

more, knowing that it obscured the metallic blood-smell just beneath her smooth flesh. It was one of the ways in which she tormented me; she knew I could smell it across a room. I tended not to breathe a lot when I was with her.

She absently pulled her peignoir up to cover her shoulder and then, realizing I was watching her, she let it slip down again with a sly smile. My fangs were beginning to slide out of their sheaths again, and I tried desperately to look away. She moved around the bed, into my field of view, and peeled the pegnoir off slowly, stroking herself as she went. Delicate teacup-sized breasts, tipped with pink—another feature she was so proud to have grown—slender waist, narrow hips. I remembered when her estrogen-sculpted body had driven me to distraction, when I would have begged to be allowed to touch her. It seemed like a long time ago. The only passion left to me now was forbidden by my faith. In desperation, I began to recite the Zavaret's Laws in my head. Thou shalt not kill save in self-defense. Thou shalt not feed save by consent, and only on one who respects the Path. Thou shalt not harm thy feeder, even if they wish it. Thou shalt not pass on the Blood save to one who has taken the vows. Thou shalt not use the Eye—

Feather paused, robe just about to fall away and uncover the rest of her body, and my train of thought derailed. Instead of exposing herself, she reached out to me and touched my cheek. The delicate blue veins in her wrist brushed my clenched jaw. "Don't you want it?" She whispered. "Of course you do. I can tell you do. You're hard as a rock—above and below." She pressed her fingers against my lips, feeling the fangs through them, and laughed her tinkly laugh again. Then her other hand let the robe drop, a flutter of silk to the floor, and she turned on her heel. I caught one glance at her groin, a hardening bulge through black silk panties, and then she left the room in momentary triumph.

I dug my clawlike nails into her pillows and thrust my hips vainly into the mattress. I would not give in. Would not. Oh, gods. . . . Thou shalt not kill save in self-defense. Thou shalt not feed save by consent, and only on one who respects the Path. . . .

I don't remember how I managed to miss the entire vampire hysteria. Of course I don't remember much about my former life, so it stands to reason, but I must have worked pretty hard at self-enforced blindness considering three of my friends disappeared over it. I do remember vaguely the warnings on TV, the documentaries about the spread of the terrible HCARVV virus, the legislation requiring bodies to be observed for three days after death. Then Lyri vanished without a trace, and rumors went that she had been discovered and imprisoned, that her lover Tess was harassing the D.A., trying to find out what had happened to her, that Tess eventually disappeared too. I knew that all vampires were being forced into treatment programs or imprisoned for the good of the country. I even heard that the vampire treatment drug, Vrykozine, had a street value now, but I didn't pay attention to politics. At least, not until I ran into Ramon in the drugstore.

Ramon had been my lover for three years. We'd broken up amicably when he went off to get his master's degree, but here he was, back in town and at the Band-Aid rack. Everyone avoided him like the plague, and I could see why. He stank, like something that had died and was rotting, and his face was gray and lined. He smiled, briefly, when he saw me, and his gums were blackened and receding from yellowed teeth. He ducked his head, then, and I guessed that my expression had been one of horror.

Some shred of decency in me realized at once what had happened and forced me to approach him, to greet him as if nothing had happened, to hold my breath and give him a quick hug as if he was still Ramon, my ex-lover. Which he was. I recall, now, how thin he was, how brittle he seemed in my quick embrace.

I asked him out to coffee, and then at his expression regretted the stupidity of my error. Not reminding me that he probably didn't eat food any more, he said something quietly about how they wouldn't let him into a restaurant. A walk in the park then, I suggested, a queer feeling gathering in my solar plexus, and he agreed to that.

It was the Vrykozine, he explained, the drug that he was forced by law to take, that made him look and smell the way he did. "It's that or go springing for people's throats like a madman," he told me wearily from beneath his dark glasses and fedora. It had been an overcast day, so he was fairly safe from the sun. "Or so they tell me. I wasn't given the chance to find out for myself."

I told him about my new job and my new lover, Feather the transsexual dominatrix. About how in love I was, about how I was going to go back to school like he had always said I should; Feather, who was wealthy from old family money, was going to send me. He listened, smiled his painful smile, and before we parted he gave me a warning.

"Whatever you do," he said to me, "don't kill yourself. Don't take risks, like I did. Stay away from fast cars, OD'ing, fights. You can't afford to die now, with the political situation the way it is. Stay alive as long as you can."

It didn't occur to me what he'd been saying until much later, after he, too, had disappeared. Until the camps were started, and the ovens. It didn't occur to me that HCARVV was transmitted blood-to-blood, that my ex-lover had been trying to protect me. And then it was far too late.

I was tied to the great dark carved bedstead and Feather was straddling me, her perfect round ass rubbing against my hardness. I *was* hard, in spite of myself; she'd made sure of that. I strained in the bonds and desperately tried to force my fangs back into their sheaths with my tongue, which only resulted in me biting it. She laughed at me and drew a thin sharp stiletto, like a gleaming icicle, from her cleavage. I stared at its point as if hypnotized. She ran it along her breasts, down her arm, across her wrist, and then paused. I could hear the intake of breath as she braced herself for the cut. Oh, please, let me look away, let me look away! The metallic scent filled the room as the tiny scarlet trickle started down her hand.

She held it over me, teased me. I moaned as the drops hit my chest, the hunger tore at me. *Thou shalt not kill save in self-defense.* . . . Oh gods, help me. "You want it," she said. "So take it. Go ahead. It's fresh. Delicious."

I turned my head and tears leaked from my eyes; bitter-smelling, bitter-tasting, they were composed of the clear plasma I lived on, that Feather got for me on the black market. If I had been feeding on people, they would be blood tears.

"You're such a monk," she said, half amused, half exasperated. Then she backed up and mounted herself on my hard cock, using the part of me that I had given her, taking her pleasure in my helpless sobbing. The circle of her greased sphincter seemed to throb and pulse its way down my shaft, until I could feel her perfect smooth ass touching my scrotum; she adjusted her position and began to fuck herself on me, using me like an animated dildo. "Move your hips," she snarled. "You can do that much for me, you useless prick." There was almost an affectionate edge to her mockery.

I could do it, and I did, pumping in the long slow rhythm I knew she liked, as much motion as my bonds would let me. She threw back her head, her long dark hair cascading over her shoulders, and braced her hands on my shoulders. Her cut wrist still oozed, a little, mere inches from my face. I turned my head desperately to the side, avoiding it, more aware of it than anything else. Its scent made me even harder, making my breath saw in and out through my mouth, making my fists clench in their bonds. My willpower was leaking away like water through a sieve, and I turned my head slowly, one centimeter at a time, fighting every step of the way. Feather was gasping in pleasure above me as I rammed into her, wriggling on my cock with a delicious motion. Her own organ, largely shrunk from hormone treatments, was for once as hard as my own and rubbing against my belly.

Her blood had trickled down onto my shoulder; my eyes were too watery to see it, but I could smell it like a bright track in my brain. Then, just as my self-discipline was stretched to the last centimeter, she lifted herself off me and grabbed the headboard of the bedstead, moving herself forward to shove her genitals in my face. I opened my mouth automatically, well-trained by years of this routine, and she plunged in.

It was only a little less temptation than before. Heightened by the tease of fresh blood, my mind read her cock in my mouth like a mother's nipple, a popsicle full of nourishment, a potential gush of life. I could smell the blood engorgement through the thin skin sliding past my canines, and it took all my strength to keep my jaw rigid, to keep from biting down. Only the thought that she had forgotten about her game, that she wouldn't be expecting this, that I might displease her, stopped me. Somehow my feverish brain managed to edit out the fact that I might kill her.

It was a good, thing, in all, that she came after about four thrusts, and pulled away immediately.

I cried, tears leaking from my eyes. She glanced at me in satisfaction, not understanding the closeness of my inner battle. Playing with fire. Sighing and rubbing her breasts with sensuous post-orgasmic glow, she got off the bed and glanced at the clock.

"I'm going to get a drink," she said. "You can make yourself come, or not, as you please. After I go." She grabbed her peignoir and swept out of the room.

The second she had left, I broke. My mouth went straight for the smear of blood still on my shoulder, fangs out and eyes blazing. I couldn't quite reach it with my tongue, and my body spasmed in frustration, snapping the chain attached to my wrist. My mouth hit my shoulder so fast that my fangs sank an inch into my own bicep; there was a clean, searing pain, and I came, hips jerking and clear fluid arcing into the air like a fountain.

It's strange. In the movies, it's always a few dedicated mortals who wipe out the powerful vampires before they become a plague and rule the earth. No one else believes them, and they win only by the barest margin. Who would have thought that we'd be so easy to control, to wipe out, when the government really put its mind to it? That we would prove so ultimately fragile in the end?

I died from a street bashing. There were still a few queer-bashers in the world, although most of the public preoccupation was with vampires, the new Public Enemy. Someone read Feather as we were leaving a club, thought she was a drag queen, and attacked. I got in the way to protect her and got half my ribs broken, one lung punctured. Feather wanted to take me to a hospital, but in a sudden flash of insight I remembered Ramon and realized that a public hospital might not be the best place to (possibly) wake up. I knew in that moment it was going to happen. I don't know how, since there's not even a medical test that can determine what solid citizen has HCARVV dormant in their system, waiting to be triggered by brain death. But somehow, lying there in the taxi gasping in pain, I knew, and I had Feather take me home. I lay in agony on my bed for a long time before my lungs filled with blood and my body gave up the fight.

But not the ghost.

When I woke up, there was a stranger sitting in my room. I still don't know how they found me, unless it was the Zavaret's powers that somehow sensed the first breath of a new vampire. "Take a shower and clean up," the quiet, dark-skinned man said to me, "and then come with me. The Zavaret wants to see you."

The Zavaret, the Holy Damned One. All you'd have to do to be totally convinced to join DarkMother's Children was to look her once in the eyes. I couldn't have resisted. She taught us the Path, the Way of discipline, the Rules. "You're not doing this for the authorities," she'd say, nailing me with that sea-colored saint's gaze behind vampire eyes. "Nor, for that matter, the great teeming mass of humanity. You're doing this for your own soul. If we're going to live as long as gods, we have a responsibility to act like gods, not animals."

Then the underground temple had been raided and the Zavaret captured, and I barely escaped with my life. And I came, of course, back to Feather. There seemed nowhere else to go.

Feather was on her knees before me, blowing me. Her purpled lips closed on my cock as she clutched my calves, going all the way to the root. I tangled my fingers in her hair and moaned, pushing down on her head, the way she liked it. Once in a while, when she'd done something that actually made her feel guilty, she liked to be punished, to be forced to suck me or to be taken from behind on all fours. I wondered briefly if she was feeling sorry for her blood-torment of me, even though I'd implicitly consented, I'd agreed to do anything she wanted once she'd taken me in. I didn't know; she'd just walked in and dropped to her knees.

I knew what it was that she was trying for, though; some kind of absolution. I took a firmer grip on her hair and shoved my hips harder into her face, making her choke slightly. Then I pulled out, made her take my balls in her generous mouth, the entire scrotum. She licked them obediently, without a verbal command; she knew the drill. I rammed my cock back into her hot, wet mouth, pressing her face to my pubic bone and holding it there until tears leaked from her eyes and one fist pounded the floor in spite of herself. Then I judged she'd had enough, and it was time to come. She swallowed what there was of my clear fluid and pulled away, gasping. "Was that what you wanted?" I asked quietly.

She sat panting on the floor, one hand pressing against her heart. There was something different about her as she curled there, no edge of pleasure to what she'd done. No arrogance to her attitude; she was almost hesitant. "Tonio?" she said in an almost little-girl voice, and what could I do but take her in my arms? She buried her black-satin head on my shoulder. "I did it, Tonio," she said, and my heart thudded against my rib cage. "I couldn't wait for you. I did it."

I turned her head gently to the side, saw the already mostly faded indentations on her throat. How could I have missed that white-lightning scent of another vampire on her flawless skin? "Who?" I said thickly, and for one moment I wanted to throw the Path out the window. It should have been me, it should have been my blood she'd taken, coursing through my lover. How could I have been so stupid? Then I almost laughed, realizing that I would be ridiculous to beat myself up for not infecting her just as I've been beating myself up for wanting to.

She shrugged and wrapped her arms around herself. "It doesn't matter. Let's just say you're not the only pet vampire hiding in someone's basement." There was an attempt at humor in her voice, but something was frightening her.

"Are you all right? He wasn't on Vrykozine, was he? No, of course not, your bite marks are already healed, if he'd been on Vrykozine you'd be a gushing corpse—" I was babbling. She silenced me with a finger to my lips and then kissed me, fiercely, hungrily.

"I have to decide how I'm going to do it," she said. "And I want you to help me. Please, Tonio."

But you already—"Help you to what?"

"Die, of course." She smiled and looked away. "It'll have to be soon . . . within the next year, I suppose. As soon as I get my surgery, which will be this spring."

"What!" I leap up, my throat constricting with

unscreamed words. "You c-can't—Feather, my god! Do you know what they'll do to you if they find out? They'll put you in a freaking incineration chamber and burn you!" And then they'll do the same to me, if you're not here to hide and protect me.

I watched tears fill her eyes. "Damn you, Tonio," she whispered. "I'm forty-one years old. How much longer do you think this body is going to be able to look like this? I don't want to spend eternity wrinkled and graying. I think I'd rather die." She reached out a hand to me, pleading. This was a Feather that I'd never seen before. "There's no one else I trust to help me do it—to teach me what it's like. And then we'll be peers, we'll be equal. We can be together forever." When I didn't take her hand, she dropped it. "I don't want to have to do it alone, but I will if I must, you know that."

I knew it. "On two conditions," I said. "First, we leave the country. I don't know where. We'll find somewhere. Second, you take the vows I've taken and follow the Path."

Now her eyes flashed fury. "You and your damned religion!" she spat. "All it's done is come between us and make us unhappy, and now you won't be with me unless I follow it? I am not cut out to be a nun, Tonio! I won't deny myself pleasures. And now I know," her hand went to her throat, and then, imperceptibly, to her lips, her teeth, "what a pleasure it is!"

"It's not about denial," I said miserably. "It's about self-control, and consent—"

"Consent!" she snapped. "That's a very nice pipe dream, but we're being hunted down in the streets, and as you pointed out, burned! Your precious Zavaret is in prison for life, being experimented on! If you think there's anyone out there so untouched by propaganda that they'd even conceive of allowing us to feed on them, you're a bigger fool than I thought you were." Feather turned away, her hair like a black silk veil over her face. "Besides, I can think of a few people who are nothing more than a waste of space, that nobody'd cry over if they disappeared."

I felt cold all over, as cold as I'd felt when I'd first awoken to my new life. Frozen. I left the room like a puppet, my limbs like a marionette's, obeying my will without feeling. Thou shalt not kill save in self-defense. A terrifying picture was forming in my mind, a picture of what Feather would become if I left her now, left her to die and awake to the hunger, the sensuous red drooling hunger that drove you like an animal to the streets, if you weren't careful. No one should be forced to go through that alone. And yet, and yet . . . I couldn't stay to watch her reject everything I had come, at great cost, to value. Would I condemn my lover, or myself?

Three months until her surgery, the vaginoplasty she'd saved up for and longed for. Three months and then what? She was waiting, giving me time; I could sense her mood in the rooms behind me. She was hoping I'd come around, that religious fanaticism would not prove more important than her. If it was you, I could almost hear her say, I'd do it for you.

I'd do it for you.

It was night outside. I hadn't seen the sky in nearly four months. Night, and no vampires prowled the pavement. Only police. The predators hid, trembling, from an even greater and more unfeeling predator. The state.

My hand was on the thick drapes that hid our private

world from the watchful eyes of Big Brother. I was just
about to lift them, to open the window and breathe the
night air, when the phone rang. Three rings, four, five.
Feather wasn't answering; I got the feeling she'd locked herself in the bathroom. Crying?

I picked up the phone, knowing it was the single most
dangerous thing I could do. It didn't seem to matter any
more. "Hello?" I said thickly. "Feather's nest."

"Tonio?" The voice seemed from a century past. "Tonio,
is that you? I thought we'd find you there, after you disappeared, but we never got anything but the answering
machine."

Fireworks shot through my blood and I was suddenly
very, very awake. "Ramon!"

"Shh! Are you sure this line isn't tapped?"

"I'm not sure of anything these days, Ramon. Just keep
talking, please! Don't hang up on me!" I clung to the receiv-
er like a lifeline.

"All right. I'll make it fast. You want out, Tonio?"

"Out?" Out of the country. "Yes!" I hissed, before I could
start thinking and change my mind.

"A car will come by for you at two-thirty. It's the last bus
out for, I don't know, maybe a long time, maybe ever. Can
you be ready that soon?"

Less than four hours. I twisted in the wind for a moment,
agonized. "Yes. Yes, I'll be ready."

"It'll be a hearse. You climb in the back, shut yourself in
the coffin. Don't look at the driver." A quick pause. "Where
we are, there's no need for the drugs," he said. He sounded
as if he wanted to say more, was struggling with himself.

"I understand," I said, although I didn't, quite. The phone
went dead and I turned toward the back of the house.

Feather was sleeping, curled up among the silk sheets

like a china doll. The tracks of tears marked her cheeks, smudged trails in her mascara. How long had I been standing at that window? I touched her hair, her shoulder. She moved slightly in her sleep. Don't think, I told myself. Don't feel. Don't look. Two lives so far, up in smoke. How many more?

I wrote her a letter, in eyebrow pencil, on the mirror. "I'll come back for you," I wrote. "Try to remember to be kind, Feather. My love for eternity, Antonio." I wasn't sure how much of it was true.

"We will be everywhere," the Zavaret told us, an hour before they came to take her away. "We will be in the streets, in the jungles, in the desert. We will go into the places where mortals would die and save who needs saving. We will go into the places of plague and tend their wounds, for we alone are safe. We will go into the places of famine and trade blood for food, for medical care. We have given up our right to reproduce in order that our neighbors' grandchildren may have a place to stand. We who have been damned will be the angels of mercy, whether they will believe it or not."

I wait on the street corner, breathing the night air for the first time in months. The headlights of an oncoming hearse illuminate the night. The air smells of smoke, the burning ground, the crematorium of our lives.

And when the smoke clears, we will be everywhere.

Would You Live For Me?

Mary Anne Mohanraj

. . . a mythical creature of varied powers and weaknesses. Peasant wisdom claims that garlic worn at the wrists and neck and wreathed around doors and window frames will ward off the monster, and that the touch of a cross or Christian holy water will burn the undead skin, as acid would burn a human. They cannot bear the light of the sun, and the merest touch of it will sear them down to bone. Lastly, their only source of true nourishment is fresh and bubbling blood, preferably human and healthy, though they are inhuman, and cannot be infected by human ills. Among their other compensations are extremely long, if not immortal, lifespans and superhuman strength . . .

"Peter?" The voice that echoed down the long hall of the apartment trembled. The stocky figure bent over the stack of heavy books lifted his fair head quickly.

"Yes, Ian? Do you need something?"

"No, I'm fine." A pause, and the voice continued, slightly weaker. "Are you coming to bed soon?" Peter's heart twisted in his chest at the high quaver in that once-solid voice.

"A little longer, love. I'm going to do a bit more reading, and then I thought I'd take a walk before turning in. If you'd like to join me . . ." Peter fell silent, knowing the answer. In the last weeks, Ian had grown bitter at the need for the wheelchair and seldom ventured beyond the bedroom, relying on Peter for his food and medicines. He still managed to get to the shower, but it was an arduous trek, and once there, his frail, sunken body simply leaned against the wall while Peter washed him.

The voice whispered down the hallway, "No, I'm pretty tired. I think I'll just go to sleep. Wake me when you come in."

"Of course," Peter promised, knowing that he wouldn't have the heart. The voice was silent, and Peter bent again over his stack of musty books, dredged from used bookstores and almost-deserted libraries. He was no scholar—a carpenter who worked more with his hands than his head, but his hands had been all but useless for months now, good only for taking what care they could of Ian's swiftly decaying body. If the books could not help him, Peter was lost, so he had strained his eyes for months, desperately seeking the answers he hoped were hidden in the yellowed pages.

. . . can often be found in cemeteries, for they must sleep surrounded by their native earth, or they will not rest . . .

The moonlight was bright, and Peter's blond beauty shone in it as he walked, restlessly, in the shadows of ancient mausoleums. Encased in a long coat too heavy for the warm summer night, he strode back and forth, pausing occasionally to poke at the weeds above a gravesite with a wooden cane, searching for a break in the grass, a hint that the grave might contain more than it seemed to. His search went unrewarded, and eventually he sank to rest on a stone plaque that lay low to the ground and buried his face in his hands.

"Why so sad, pretty boy?" A woman's voice, low and laughing. Peter's head jerked up and there, kneeling before him, was a pale young woman. Silver hair flowed smoothly down her back and across one naked shoulder, and a silver ankh hung on a chain around her bare neck. Black leggings and leather boots would have completed the effect, were it not for the white crop tank she wore, decorated with a bright yellow smiling face, and "Have a nice day" inscribed below. Despite the incongruous top, Peter knew that he'd found what he'd been seeking. He froze, knowing the urgency, too frightened to speak.

"No answer? Of course not. Let us see what I can deduce of you, my beauty, since I have robbed you of speech. Why would an exceedingly handsome young man like yourself—so strong, so muscular—be haunting my cemetery, for seven nights in a row, with such a sad and sorrowful face?" She raised a slender hand and reached out to run a black-nailed finger along the curve of Peter's cheek, stopping only briefly at the collar of the coat, before reaching underneath to draw out what hung on a heavy chain around his neck.

"Garlic and crosses, my sweet?" She laughed. "I know a delectable recipe for garlic and rosemary chicken—not very filling for me, of course, but the taste is sublime. The tales of garlic's power against my kind are just tales, I'm afraid. As for the crosses—you don't believe in their power, so I'm afraid they have no power over me. So sorry. But I do appreciate your doing your homework. It's nice to have a client who really cares. Now don't worry—this won't hurt at all. . . ."

She bent toward him, crimson lips drawing back to reveal sharp teeth. Just as her tongue licked out to taste the salt-skin above the pulsing artery of his neck, Peter managed to whisper, "Wait. . . ."

She pulled back, frowning. "Now, you shouldn't have been able to do that, my pretty one. That's what the 'look' is for, after all, to calm and freeze our clients. I won't kill you, you know, no matter what the stories say. Crude and tasteless to treat a human so—only the very young are so unrestrained, and I have not been young for millenia. So just relax—you might even enjoy it, and you'll have forgotten all about it by tomorrow." She bent forward again, but before she even touched the skin, Peter was whispering, "Please . . . oh, please. . . ."

A look of frustration crossed her face, and she stood up, her body a dark shaft in the pool of moonlight. The night suddenly grew quieter around them, as the wind died down and the small animal noises disappeared. "Don't irritate me, lovely boy. Even if I let you live, the blood-taking doesn't have to be pleasant. . . ."

Peter was silent again, and the moment hung between them, low and heavy. One, two, three, four seconds passed like hours, and then she laughed again, her mood shimmering and shifting like the moonlight.

"All right, talk! Whatever's bothering you, it must be tremendously strong for your emotions to overcome the 'look.' But your story had best be a good one. And I'll have to take this . . . an ingenious version of a wooden stake, by the way." She reached out and pulled the cane from his hand, then settled onto the grass, leaning against a nearby gravestone. Peter's voice was suddenly free again, and after a long breath the words spilled out, stumbling over themselves in their anguished plea.

. . . avoid their haunts, for though they possess a unearthly beauty, these undead monsters have no soul, and therefore have nothing in them of human kindliness. There is no warmth, no pity to them, and even the most impassioned of pleadings will not sway them from their dark desires . . .

She listened, and questioned, and responded to Peter's words, and when he had finished, she paused a long moment before shrugging her response. "A very sad story, not amusing at all. And so common nowadays. . . . My little golden child, even assuming that I do possess the happy ending you so greatly desire, why should I give it to you? What can you offer me?" She tilted her head, so that the light washed against the delicate planes of her face, and waited for his answer.

Peter's hands clenched at his sides as he gave the ancient creature the answer he'd prepared. "Myself. It's all I have, all I can offer. My money, my home, my body, my life . . . my service through the centuries to come. Make me one of you as well and I will be your devoted slave, lady, if you will do this one thing for me that you could do so easily." He was trembling now, breathless with his need.

"Ah, there you're wrong." She paused, and what seemed

to be, but could surely not be, fear crossed her narrow face. A moment later she shrugged and continued. "Doing what you ask would leave a horrible taste in my mouth for weeks . . . but you are somewhat appealing. Perhaps a trial run, to see if you can please me? The grass is soft, and the night is warm. . . ." She was laughing now, a fine full laugh with head tilted back, as she watched Peter struggle to step forward, to wrap her slender body in his strong arms. He finally managed to overcome his distaste, and she whispered softly, "See, women aren't so scary. Just wait 'til you see what you've been missing all these years. . . ."

She tore the chain from his throat, briefly and terrifyingly reminding him of her unnatural strength. Then she discarded the garlic and crosses, wrapped her arms tightly around Peter, and pulled him down to the soft grass. She gently moved his hands under her top to her white breasts. He shivered slightly, and then bent to kiss her. The kiss— his first with a woman—was surprisingly sweet, though her lips were shockingly cold. A current ran between them, and without volition his hands closed on her breasts, tighter and tighter as she sucked deeply on his lips and tongue, careful not to even brush him with her teeth. She moaned encouragingly, and Peter struggled to remember what his female friends had told him—all the ways in which a man could do too much, or too little. So much depended on his pleasing this creature tonight—who was at least female, if not human.

He rubbed his rough fingers over her nipples, tentatively at first. She twisted beneath him, and Peter almost stopped . . . then he realized that she was arching up into his touch. He rubbed harder, and she slid a thigh between his, wrapped her other leg around his hips so that his left thigh pressed against the curiously smooth intersection of her legs and hips. Peter kissed down her face, along the line of neck and up to bite gently at her earlobe, teasing it as he had teased Ian's so many times. They slid against each other, her hands on his buttocks urging him on, in a motion that was not so different from ways in which he had moved before. His own sweat was rank in the air, but from her came the scent of sandalwood and soil, and while her flesh did not warm beneath his touch, he could taste the femaleness of her, the sweet musk permeating his skin.

Peter was curious now, and began to explore her body, sliding the black leggings down to her knees and laying bare the triangle of hairless flesh that lay between her thighs. She arched blindly as he did so, seeking his touch, and he denied her, amazed at his own temerity. Slow . . . slow was what women liked, or so he'd been told, and now he staked his own life and that which was so much more precious than his own life on the honesty of his friends' gossip. Slowly his fingers trailed over the sharp angles that were her body—yet not so sharp as what had become of Ian's body, as the wasting took him and the flesh melted away. Her skin was chill, but firm, and as he curved his large hands around her rounded buttocks a thrill of lust shot through Peter, shocking him with its presence and intensity.

He lowered his head, to lick circles around her belly and up to her breasts, her top now pushed high to bare their small firmness. He sucked each nipple gently, then firmly; then, as her nails sank into his back, perhaps drawing the first blood, he bit down, his own fingers digging into her soft skin, his crotch pressed hard against her thighs. Down again, and this time only a little teasing, a light dip and taste before he dove, tongue searching and prodding, and she tasted like flowers and soil and moonlight wrapped together. Though she moaned and shivered beneath him, no fluids appeared to coat her passageway, and so he licked long and hard, finally licking a finger and thrusting it deep inside her. She screamed then, and Peter thought he'd hurt her until he looked up to see the smile on her face, the fierce possessive smile that said *yes*.

And the urgency was strong in him now. He unbuttoned his jeans and pushed them down, releasing his cock into the chill night air for a moment before he slid inside her. At least by contrast she was warm and wet. He pushed up and in, and then pulled back, and this motion at least was familiar, so familiar that only a few strokes later he came, shuddering deep inside her, legs pressed hard against hers and his hands clenched deep in the soil. He collapsed on top of her, mindless for a moment. She let him rest there, silently, and it was not until he raised his head to look at her, a question in his eyes, that she smiled at him and asked, "Again?"

. . . for they are creatures of insatiable appetites . . .

They lay nestled on their sides in the shadow of a stone, her hips against his, her small left breast cradled in his long-fingered hand. He was asleep, and the small puncture wounds in his neck were barely visible in the fading moonlight. Her green eyes were opened wide, and her fingers curled around his hand, tracing lines in the skin. They lay that way an endless time, until the light of day began to creep over the eastern hills.

"Peter . . ." Her voice was surprisingly soft, and he did not answer. "Peter, it's time to go." She turned in his arms, but he only groaned. A smile stretched across her face, although something lurked beneath it. She raised a hand and raked a nail across his chest. Peter's eyes flew open, a question burning in them. Before he could ask it, she stopped his mouth with a kiss, long and sweet and sad with might-have-beens. Then she was pulling away and dressing quickly in the breaking light. "I'll come to you tomorrow night," she murmured. "Be sure that he's asleep. Drug him if you must. I make no promises—none of my kind has attempted this."

"And the price?" Peter asked. "What do you want from me in exchange?"

She pulled her top over her head and shook her hair free before turning to smile at him. "The price is paid. If it works, the two of you can buy me dinner in a century or two . . . and perhaps we'll share something more than dinner?" A sad question lingered in her eyes, but before Peter could ask her what was wrong, he blinked, and she was gone.

. . . and remember, the grave is a cold place; the coldness of the soil they sleep in will creep into the monster's skin and remain there, despite all they do to warm themselves . . .

Ian hadn't wanted to take anything to help him sleep. Peter had had to borrow their landlord's cat, bring it quietly inside, and let it walk around the bathroom for a bit. When Ian used the bathroom later, the hair set off his allergies and he started coughing, shuddering. Peter's throat tightened, but it did mean that Ian was willing to take some antihistamines . . . and within half an hour, Ian was out cold. Peter opened the window, and she flowed into the room, naked and lovely. He didn't even ask her how she'd managed that, considering they were two stories up. He didn't want to know.

They stood facing each other over Ian's bed, where he lay, curled and trusting as a child.

"Pull back the sheets," she said.

Peter hesitated—but Ian had pulled them up so tight that only his face was visible. Peter gently pulled the sheets from Ian's fingers and drew them down. She dragged in her breath and bit her lip.

"He's so ugly!"

White-hot words rose to Peter's lips and died there. To a creature made perfect in form, any human might well be ugly . . . and Ian's body was a cruel parody of what it once had been. Peter could still see the perfection of line in Ian's curving back, the hidden strength of his hands. He didn't need to show her, though.

She glanced back and forth between them. Her hands clenched and unclenched at her sides. She took a step forward, and reached down to touch Ian's chest.

"You won't . . ." Peter didn't know what he could say—everything was in her hands now, and she could do whatever she wanted, but still . . .

She shook her head. "I have no desire for your lover. I will not touch him beyond what is needful. But there is a problem."

"What?" Peter's voice broke on that one word, but he didn't care. It was too late for caring about such things.

"I cannot do this without desire. The blood will be foul; I need heat burning through me to clean it. Lie you down beside your lover. Touch me as I taste him. Keep me burning, or we will have no chance of cleansing him."

Peter nodded, and slowly stripped. He lay down on the bed and she lay down atop him, her mouth near Ian's throat. Peter's pulse quickened at the feel of her flesh on his chest, the feel of Ian's thigh against his—still, despite everything. She kissed him, and he caressed her breast, feeling the fire start to burn. Then she lifted her head.

"One more thing . . ." she said.

"Anything." What could he deny her now?

"I am Katya." She smiled, with some effort. "I thought we should be properly introduced."

Peter wondered how much danger was in this for her, after all. He wanted to ask—but she didn't want to say, and perhaps it was better that way.

"Sounds Transylvanian," he said instead.

"Ukrainian, actually." Katya smiled more genuinely then, and bent down to Ian's throat. Peter slid a hand between her thighs and began to caress her as her teeth sunk into his lover's skin and the bright blood flowed.

. . . *it is their power that is so beautiful, so sexual and irresistible to the poor mortal . . .*

The effects hadn't been immediate.

Katya had left just before dawn, and Peter had gotten up, pulled the shade closed, and then climbed back into bed. He was asleep within minutes, and had slept until nightfall. When he woke, Ian had still been asleep, and Peter had pulled back the sheet carefully. His eyes had filled with tears when he saw no change in his lover's body. He almost woke Ian then and confessed everything.

Katya had said it might take more time than usual. He had promised her he would be patient.

Now his patience was rewarded. Three weeks gone, and Ian was looking better. The difference was slight, but there was visibly more flesh on his bones. He was eating more, and keeping it down. His interest in sex had rekindled, and though Peter still refused to let Ian carry his full weight, he could feel the returning strength in Ian's body.

They made love slowly at night, and Peter kept his mouth busy all over Ian's body, along back and thighs and calves—anywhere but on Ian's own mouth. Katya had warned him that if they kissed, the fangs might extend involuntarily, and Peter wasn't ready to tell Ian what he had done—not until he was absolutely sure of the cure's potency. So Peter's mouth was most often on his lover's cock, his hands feeling the returning muscle of Ian's thighs. When Ian moaned his pleasure, his hands clenched in Peter's hair, Peter thought of Katya and prayed.

. . . as we remarked earlier, their unholy vitality can only be explained by a pact with Lucifer. Yet it is easy to see why a man might be tempted by eternal youth, health and life, though it be at the cost of his soul . . .

Peter sat cross-legged on the wide bed, watching the snow fall outside their window and carefully avoiding sight of Ian's heavy gold crucifix on the west wall. Peter still dreamed of her occasionally, though it had been several months since they'd met, and he had to resist the impulse to visit the cemetery again. He had found other streets for his nocturnal ramblings; the city was large enough that it would be months before he learned all its nighttime moods and places. Of course, he had nothing but time.

Ian stirred in the blankets, flinging one pale arm out from under the covers and across Peter's thighs. The impact woke him, and he blinked sleepily at Peter. "It's almost morning, dear. Been up all night again?"

"Mmhmmm . . ." Peter reached out to draw down the shade, as he had every dawn since that night in the cemetery. The light hurt Ian's eyes. "How are you feeling today?"

"Actually, I'm feeling wonderful." Ian spoke slowly, considering his words. "I didn't expect another remission—I didn't even expect to see Christmas this year, you know. But I feel almost *healthy* today. Perhaps we could go for a walk later? It's been so long since I've been out in the light . . ."

Ian smiled up at Peter hopefully, and Peter's heart twisted once again as he reached to pull Ian into his arms. "Of course we can go for a walk, love. I'm so glad that you're feeling better. But perhaps we should have a talk first. There's something I need to tell you . . ." . . . *and I pray that you can forgive me*, he finished silently.

The Only
Steve Eller

Brushing back the silken curtain from the bedside, I rose. The cold stone floor-tiles tingled against my bare feet as I crossed to the window, opening the bamboo shutters to glance up at the sky. An infinity of stars glittered, sprayed across a black field like shards of a shattered moon. A few wisps of dust-gray cloud drifted slowly by, like lost phantoms. The crisp night air wandered over my bare limbs, raising chill bumps. Raising my nipples, and the fine hairs at the nape of my neck.

Far below my window, a darkened landscape rolled endlessly toward a haze-shrouded horizon. Scattered through the shadowy hills were clumps of slender young trees, teak and mahogany, koa. The outside world was deathly silent except for the soft sizzle of insect wings and the distant hiss of the ocean as it broke against stone.

I turned away and moved back toward my warm bed, wondering what had become of the people who had once owned this magnificent house. It seemed it had been long ago that we'd come here, but my memory often plays tricks, perhaps unable to comfortably cradle so many years. But I was certain I had not built this place. So I must have taken it. Surely then the owners were dead, their bodies softening beneath the moist earth, or their pale bones wandering lazily over the floor of the sea.

A pity, for surely they must have loved such a beautiful place. And they must have loved one another deeply, to have chosen to be here together, so isolated from all others. A pity, but such is the way of things when there is need. I needed their house. We needed it. And need is eternal. Like hunger, like love.

I climbed onto the bed and rested on my knees, gazing down at the face of my lover. Her delicate features appeared serene in the moonlight, her pale hands folded beneath her chin, clutching the edge of the silk bedsheet to her throat like a dreaming child. Her long lashes curled atop her delicate cheeks, her eyes closed as if sleeping. But I knew she was dead. Only for a while, but no less dead.

Pain spiked out from my heart as I drew back the sheets from her still form. She was beyond perfect, an angel sculpted from the purest marble. A goddess woven of moonlight and dream. Her only flaw, a dark wound on her pallid wrist. My breath caught in my throat as I gazed at it. A void opened in my heart as I realized I had done this thing, marred her so. It had been born of need, of hunger and love. And she had offered herself willingly, even eagerly. But still the sight stung me.

I lifted her motionless arm and drew her curled fingers to my lips. I kissed them, then her cool palm, then her damaged wrist. I felt a tear wandering down my cheek as I studied the wound. The cut was deep, the bruise surrounding it an angry purplish-black. It would vanish, and heal without a trace. But the fact I had hurt her, even in throes of passion, weighed heavily on my heart. This was a creature I would die for. That I had died for, countless times.

I clasped her hand tightly to my chest as I brushed my lips up her arm and over her bare shoulder. I kissed her throat, touching the tip of my tongue to the place where her pulse once throbbed. A strange mingling of passions surged through me as I ran my lips over her breasts. I felt love, frightening in its depth, dizzying and bottomless. I felt misery for being the one who had brought cruel death to one so cherished. And I experienced shame, as if I was somehow violating her, caressing her unmoving body so. I felt like a heathen, desecrating the most sacred of temples.

But I could not help myself. Another need, lust, overcame my shame. In my fevered brain I imagined she would not mind this touching. I pictured her face, her eyes softened with love, cheeks heated with emotion. Ragged breaths flowing over her open mouth as I explored her mysteries with lips and tongue. It seemed as if she had once told me to do this very thing, to ravish her body while she slept the sleep of death. Or perhaps I had dreamed it. In the end it made no difference. Soon enough, the dream would be real again.

Sliding my tongue between her lips, I licked her cold, slick teeth. The tips of her fangs were hard and sharp, and I almost allowed them to rend my flesh, spilling my blood over her tongue. But it was too soon for that. Lacing my fingers into hers, I kissed the tip of her pointed chin, the arch of her throat, then down her breastbone to her belly. Lower still, I pressed my tongue to the soft folds between her legs.

I found a flutter of warmth there, and my heart leapt. The spark of forever still burned deep within her, waiting to blaze again.

Soon, my love, I thought. *So very soon.*

I raised myself and released her fingers. My hands fluttered over her, my thoughts drowning in adoration. She was the only. The rest of the world had faded into insignificance until only she remained. Surely somewhere beyond our tiny island millions of people teemed, humans, perhaps others like us. But they no longer mattered. Until the end of the world, she was the only.

In spite of the chill in the air, my face felt hot, as if burning with fever. The tips of my sodden hair stuck to my neck and cheeks as I nuzzled her soft skin once more. My tongue swelled in my mouth like a soaked cloth and flopped out, leaving glistening rings of saliva in my wake as I worked her chilled flesh again. My tongue slathered her body, wandering between her legs, probing deep this time, licking the tiny bite-scars that would one day vanish completely.

The veil of illusion fell away. She was not dead. A word did not exist for what she was. Silent, motionless, almost bloodless. Yet she was a thing which could not die. Perhaps, if I left her as she was, she might soften into moldy bone or fall fully into dust. Or perhaps she might remain as now. There was no way to know, and I was not anxious to learn. It was something I could never allow. For even as dust she might continue, the essence of her immortality clinging to a single arid flake until time's end. The image was maddening, of a deathless thing, alert, unable to soothe the hungers of need. I could not even conceive of permitting such a travesty.

It was nearly time. I could not resist a nip of her precious flesh, just a taste. It enflamed me, having something of her in me. For a dizzying moment my fondest wish was to have all of her within my mouth at once. To feel her entire body against my tongue.

Straddling her hips, I gazed down and saw my cock risen. An urgency bloomed in my heart as I watched the blood gathering, making me hard. The only blood in the world. With trembling fingers I brushed her face, then opened her mouth.

A cold fire. It was the only way to describe the agony in my heart as she headed for the door. I stared at the abstract pattern of moonlight on the bedroom floor, unable to bear the look in her eyes. The glaze of hunger. For another. The icy flame swirled and grew, devouring my emotions.

"Please don't go out tonight," I suddenly whispered.

I heard her hand fall on the knob and waited breathlessly for the sharp click as she turned it. But the sound never came. When I raised my eyes again, she was staring at me. Silence lingered between us for long moments. Outside our apartment window I heard the din of countless feet striking asphalt, the clutter of voices and thoughts without number.

"What did you say, my love?"

"Nothing," I replied, lowering my eyes again. "It's just that . . . nothing."

An instant later she was beside me, her hand against my cheek, lifting my face. Her tropical-sea blue eyes shimmered with concern and confusion.

"I just need to go out for a few moments." She spoke slowly, her voice soft as if trying to soothe a child. "To kill. When I come back we can. . . ."

Her voice faded away. She cupped my face as I closed my

eyes more tightly, unable to bear the things I felt. Tears streaked down my cheeks, born of some unnamable emotion. My stomach clenched. I had killed for blood two nights before and my hunger was a gnawing ache. Still, it was nothing compared to the feeling of emptiness in my heart. The depth of my misery startled me, and I struggled to understand what it meant.

Biting my lip, I forced myself to look at her again, to suffer the pain her visage caused in me. And in that instant I realized the agony I felt was love. I had always known I loved her, it was why I had sealed her in eternal flesh with my blood. But the magnitude of it became clear in that fleeting flicker of time.

Perhaps it had taken centuries of distillation for my emotions to become pure enough. But the love was absolute. A love that might only be measured in pain, in the ache of separation, in the eternity of longing. In the realization that there would never be surcease were it to be lost. The profundity awed me. I wished to die in her arms at that moment, to find a way to do it without causing her pain. I desperately wanted to flee, and never look on her again, rather than someday learn that she had died. But my traitorous muscles betrayed me, and I was unable to move.

Her fingertips lightly brushed my cheeks, wiping away my tears. I shivered as her arm closed around my shoulders.

"What is it," she whispered in my ear. "Tell me."

I knew the things in my head would never make sense if spoken. There were no words to make her understand. She would question my strange feelings, appease them, and she would be right. But the poignant emotions had moved beyond right and wrong. They were absolutes. I had no language to express them, so I said what I could.

"Don't leave me tonight."

"I wish only to stay with you. But it's been days. I have to kill tonight. I need the blood."

I felt my insides crumbling, curling like dying fingers. The thought of her leaving me, even for a short while, was excruciating. The thought of her mouth on another was crushing. The image of a stranger's blood flowing through her veins was unbearable.

"No!"

I quivered, shocked at the vehemence in my voice. Her eyes widened within her precious face, filled with a desperate hunger and a deep sorrow. I raised my wrist to her mouth.

"Take mine," I whispered. "Only mine."

Her brow furrowed, and I wondered if she thought I'd gone insane. But her trembling lips parted, her tongue moistening my wrist. She closed her eyes as her teeth pierced me. The drawing of her mouth was unendurable, but I swooned as if in ecstasy. I was dying for my lover. Dying for love. The ultimate sacrifice, the ultimate expression of devotion.

As the blood surged from my body, I had a revelation. That this was the summit of existence. That I was the only blood she would ever need, as she would be the only blood I would ever taste again. The hollow, chaotic world outside our window vanished, until there was only the two of us. In perfect symmetry.

"Forever," I thought to her. "Until the end of the world, only this."

Her mind resisted, weakly, swathed in its tapestry of blood lust. But I kept thinking the images to her as I tumbled into cold darkness. A vision of her passing the blood back to me when she chose to. Begging that she hold it within her as long as she could, purifying it with her heart.

The final image was of the two of us, locked in an eternal, unbroken circle. Nothing else in the world. Only.

"We will find a place," I thought. "Where there are no others."

Darkness enveloped me and I welcomed it. It seared, like a cold fire, and I eagerly became ash.

Arching my back, I lowered myself to her lips. They seemed so pale against my blood-flushed cock, the chill of her flesh crackling through my sensitive skin like strands of lightning. With one hand I tilted her head so her tongue was directly underneath me. With the other I opened a quick gash in my penis, the brilliant blood twisting, spattering into her mouth.

Almost at once I felt the heat blooming in her cheeks, surging down her throat toward her dormant heart. I heard a soft hissing as her vessels expanded, carrying my blood throughout her undying body. Tiny ripples pulsated across her flesh, as the blood, our blood, resurrected her. My heart raced at the thought of her rebirth, and the blood flowed faster into her mouth.

Heart battled mind. Love warred against the will to live. Then the fighting became more complex. My rational mind ordered me to stop, before I was drained, while my emotions begged me to continue. My flesh, longing to be eternal, pleaded with me to reclaim the blood, while the rest of my body longed to melt into her mouth and trickle down her throat.

But all thought vanished into mist as her eyes opened. Our gasps came as one. Her throat shuddered, expanding to swallow all the blood in her mouth. Her lips closed around me, holding me in an unbreakable bond. I felt the scrape of her teeth, widening the wound, her tongue rolling back the tattered edges of skin. My vision blurred, and I felt my eyes skittering as she began to suckle.

My limbs became light and numb. Her lips were like fire against my skin, her hands burning as they rose and locked around my buttocks, crushing me in her fatal embrace. Waves of bliss and pain swept through me. My undead body was unable to orgasm, so I remained at the verge for what seemed an eternity as she worked me with her blazing tongue and lips.

My body lingered at the edge of climax, the pain softening into numbness. My mind teetered on the brink of vertigo, a dark void waiting for me when I fell. I would fall, as I had so many times before. When I finally tumbled into the abyss, my heart and mind rejoined, rejoicing in the knowledge that my blood had fed her and filled her. That no blood but mine coursed through her veins. And never would. Her blood now. Our blood. The only blood.

Though I still descended into darkness, I felt her lift me and lower me onto the bed, a weightless thing. I wanted to cry out in loss as her lips released me, but my body seemed distant, refusing my command. Her white-hot mouth touched me again, sprinkling kisses over my chest and throat.

It seemed as if I looked down at myself lying on the bed at the same time I experienced her mouth on me. It was a bizarre sensation, but familiar. She passed her fingers over my eyes, gently closing my lids. Then she pulled the sheets up to my chin. They felt cool against my chest.

"Soon my love," she whispered in my ear. "I will die for you."

I wondered if I was dreaming as I watched her rise and drift soundlessly across the stone floor to the window. The night breeze lifted her hair, swirling it around her flushed cheeks. Moonlight glistened along the curves of her perfect angel's body, and I longed to have her against my lips once more. But I knew I could not. Not until the blood was mine again.

Her arms rose as she turned back toward the bed, fingers brushing the tangles from her long honey-gold hair. I hungered in disembodied agony as her nipples hardened in the night breeze.

"Sleep my love," she whispered, eyes brimming with moonlight. "Until the end of time, you are the only."

The scene shimmered as if tears clouded my vision. But I felt her weight, her warmth, as she climbed back onto the bed. I wanted to touch her once more, to taste her. I longed for the blood to be in me again as desperately as I wished her to hold the blood within her forever, heating it with her precious life. Our blood. The only.

Initiation Into *Club Sanguis*

Renée M. Charles

"Sorry, never heard of no 'Kikak'. . . But I got a few openings, in case you're interested yourself—" the strip club manager's eyes moved down my torso, as his Old Fashioned glass did an ice-clinking jitterbug in his left hand, while he took puffs on his cigar with pursed lips that caressed the wet end of the stogie like a blood-engorged clit. Stepping backward, I dug around in my bag for the photo of Elita Aldora I'd taken from her album that morning.

Setting his glass on the bartop with an audible clank! he took the photo from me, sliding a quick, blunt fingertip along my palm and wrist while pulling Elita's image his way. His finger was slippery cold, leaving a moisture trail that glinted in the joint's alternately dim and bright lighting. Twenty feet away, an afternoon shift girl—less well endowed, nowhere near as pretty as an evening shift dancer (a given at every club I'd visited so far; one opening callow manager said, "Why waste the good stuff on lunch break crowds?") gracelessly wrapped a skinny arm around the obligatory dancing pole, then high kicked her opposite leg up until her foot was level with her head. A shiny hourglass of reflective pink satin covered her crotch, held in place with glitter elastic that matched her pasties.

None of the ten or twelve men sitting in the nearly empty club made a motion to dig a fiver out of their pockets.

"My offer stands . . . for you and your friend," the manager said between nursing sucks of his cigar, as he stared at the five-by-seven greedily, as if trying to suck Elita's image off the very paper.

Not that I blamed him. My new roommate was an eyeful—lithe, well-rounded, semi-almond dark eyes common to all filipinas, but taller than usual, close to five-seven or eight. In her studio photo, Elita wore closed-toe mules that rose up another four inches . . . and not much else. A thong bikini barely covered her plump mons, and the matching bra was little more than strings of coiled fabric criss-crossing her well-defined collar bones and bisecting her breasts—the circle of fabric which covered each nipple seemed an afterthought on the designer's part.

But Elita's hair was her best feature . . . thick raven black, cascading in luxuriant waves down her long neck and over her rounded shoulders . . . hair I longed to run my fingers through each time I saw her, each time her hair slid smoothly over her even smoother flesh—the same hair that smelled so strongly of other people, when she came home from her club job, in that unnamed strip joint of hers. . . .

Hence, my trek from strip joint to strip joint listed in a torn-out NYC Yellow Page, searching for the place where she danced under the nom-de-plume "Kikak" . . . but despite her exquisite looks, and that name, no one seemed to have heard of her. Yet my room-mate went somewhere each night, body ritualistically slathered from forehead to soles in that tangy-sweet lotion she kept hidden in her room, and wearing that trenchcoat of hers—she carried no books, despite her claim of being a fellow college student, nor did she arrive home smelling of burger grease—but each morning when she click-clacked back to our apartment, she carried a subtle odor of mingled aftershaves and perfumes on her body.

And the wads of crumpled bills she pulled out of her pockets hinted at something more profitable than slinging hash or giving a night school prof a quickie . . . but yet, when I'd ask her where she worked, she'd roll her eyes, and shake her head until her Bettie-Page bangs arranged themselves in frothy curls over her brow, them say, "A place you wouldn't enjoy visiting . . . not a place for a good little college girl like you," only her voice was so warm, so friendly, there was no spite or sarcasm intended.

Truly, she honestly thought of me as "a good little college girl" . . . she made no advances, said nothing salacious, did nothing to pique my interest in her (as if oblivious that my interest had been more than piqued—it'd been teased, abused, and taunted mercilessly). Just paid her share of the rent, in cash that carried the subtle scent of perfume, sweat, and musky secretions from her body, as if it had rested close in a tight G-string.

Ostensibly, I *was* Jill College; attended classes, took a weekend field trip monthly for Art History, dutifully did term papers in the apartment, rather than lugging my laptop to the nearest coffee shop and plugging in there . . . but thanks to different schedules, Elita had no reason *to* believe otherwise about me.

Conversely, Elita gave me little reason to believe her—I'd advertised for a student roommate, and she seemed the right age during the informal interview, but when she failed to bring any books or computer when moving in, I wondered what she was studying—and where.

She'd been more forthcoming about her job; considering that her wardrobe consisted of costumes smaller than a bandanna *with* a hem, adorned with enough sequins and heat-pressed rhinestones to cover RuPaul from neck to behind (front and back), all it took was a questioning glance at her closet to elicit a explanation:

"I studied native dance since I was a girl in LA—a lot of my people settled there—but there's not much call for filipina dancers here or there . . . I'm limber, I do splits and everything, so I figured 'Why not?' The money's good, and the club owner is always thrilled to see me—I get treated very, very well at the Club. . . ."

Remembering her speech as I alternately watched the plain dancer hump her glistening pole on-stage, and her boss devour Elita's photo with smoke-hazed eyes, something hit me—she'd definitely said "Club" with a capital "C." None of the places I'd been to had "Club" in the title—all of their names were far more explicitly exotic.

Tapping my hip with Elita's photo, the manager asked, "You do splits? Your roomie? I'm always open to new talent—"

Taking the photo, I asked, "These afternoon or evening openings?"

I knew what he'd say before he said it, but right then, I needed to confirm my knowledge that Elita would never return my interest in her with an true passion, or honest-ly—and, in so doing, confirm the silliness of my quest, my need to watch Elita give herself visually to all those hun-gering men (or women):

"Oh, they're for both . . . you could keep your evenings free—"

Once he'd seen Elita, the man didn't have to make an offer to me. Or so I kept telling myself. . . .

Club owners eleven through thirteen didn't offer me a job, but did grow glassy-eyed and giddy over Elita. Number four-teen was gay, seemingly in business for the money only, but then again, only he understood my true reason for pound-ing pavement on a steamy late May afternoon, Elita's photo shoved in my bag, as he handed it back to me, saying, "Good luck finding her roost, kiddo . . . birds of a feather—excuse the cliché, dear—usually stay within the flock, though. Even . . . if the plumage is a bit different, eh?"

If Elita hadn't been out of town, visiting her family, I sup-pose I never would've begun my rather silly quest, but since my family had no interest in seeing me lately, I'd stayed on in our apartment. Summer courses were starting soon, and Elita was staying on all summer, because of her job. During those first few nights alone, her absence gnawed at me; no click-clack of heels on the tile floor, no more ever-changing yet uncannily similar scent of sweet cologne clinging to her, lingering in her wake, no more listening to her shower off that clinging, vaguely iridescent lotion off her sweat-sheened body (especially when I'd stand outside the closed door, listening to the splatter of jetting water off her taut skin). . . .

The longer she was gone, the more vivid my imaginings of her became; I pictured her standing on a bright-lit stage, embracing that ubiquitous brass pole with a passion made visual, as the crowd focused only on her melon-taut breasts, gently rounded hips, and slightly convex belly, waiting eagerly for her to skitter close to the edge of the stage, so they could pull aside her G-string and shove rolls of money in there, crinkled green faux penises, pushed down deep by probing fingertips—only, my visions were distant, out of focus from the haze of smoke wafting up from the tables; I didn't dare come closer, not as a solo woman . . . no man would stand for someone like me edging him away from the stage.

And, true to the sound of her name, I imagined Elita doing high kicks, revealing the smooth outer edge of her mons with each lifting-high of her long, lean legs, but that's where my fantasy ended. I couldn't make her reveal all of herself, even though she'd hinted that the Club dancers did go totally nude. . . .

But unless her Club was downtown, or in another part of the city entirely, either Elita wasn't an exotic dancer at all, but a street girl, or . . . perhaps I *had* gone to the wrong clubs. Perhaps I should've stayed within the flock to begin with . . . but the thought of her dancing in a lesbian bar was far too exotic for me to even begin to imagine. I had an idea of what men did in strip clubs, but I also knew that women were far more imaginative. . . .

Naturally, I figured out the lesbian bar possibility right before Elita was due home from LA . . . and me with no NYC Yellow Pages in the apartment. But there was that phone booth three blocks away, the one I'd ripped the other page from . . . in my eagerness, I slammed my door too loudly; as I raced down the hallway, one of my neighbors—the old man with the silvery-clear stubble on his many chins, and the hearing aid poking out of one long-lobed ear—shuffled out of his apartment in his moccasins with the frayed lacings, and said, "You're full of vim—'spose you been gettin' a good night's sleep too lately, huh?"

"Oh, I'm always a hard sleeper, but I'm glad you're sleeping well," I said, noticing that the old guy was less bleary eyed, more alert. . . .

"Lucky girlie . . . me, a roach belches, I'm eyes open, oogling the ceiling . . . lately, all this flappy-flappy on the fire escape over there—" he pointed in the direction of the hall fire escape east of us "—and that squawkin'. . . 'kaaa-*kak*'! Like some damn ocean bird . . . been happening for weeks now, flappy-flap then 'kaaa*kak*'! and even though it don't happen again all night, I can't fall back asleep. . . . Oh, I guess I *do*, but it ain't no *restful* sleep. . . .

After he shuff-shuffed back into his apartment, I hurried down the stale-smelling hallway toward the fire-escape window. The railings beyond were flaked and rusted, and the whole thing wiggled slightly under a firmly shaking hand, but the condition of the iron edifice was of little importance to me once I noticed the greasy length of horizontal railing . . . which felt and smelled similar to the lotion Elita used. . . .

Climbing back into the building, I rubbed my fingertips and thumb against each other, savoring the barely perceptible oily residue trapped between them. The lotion's texture was similar to that of the better sex lubricants sold in those adult shops in the Village—which stayed open all night long. . . .

None of the lotions or cremes sold in the sex toys and accessories shop I visited that evening were exactly like Elita's silky-fine lotion, but I did find two which—when a daub of each was rubbed into my palm, mingling their distinctive scents—closely doubled the smell, if not the texture, of Elita's private lotion. And both were colorless, just as hers was. . . .

During the subway ride home, I hugged my bagged purchases close to me, letting the growing heat in my torso and upper arms leech into the plastic bottles, as I pictured Elita picking up her unlabeled glass bottle and uncapping it only to pause a second while smelling it, before shaking her head (she had spent a long time in smog-clogged LA, so surely her sense of smell was off-kilter) and slathering it on anyhow. And even though it wasn't possible, I fancied that the heat of my body still radiated from that lotion, so that she was entirely coated with my warmth, my spent body heat. . . .

Before leaving, Elita told me that this was to be a complete vacation—so all of her skimpy bathing suits stayed in that closet. In fact, she promised that she wouldn't even work on a tan. . . .

So, since the lotion was part of her work, I doubted that she'd brought it to California. She never used the lotion in the bathroom, but instead emerged glistening and lusciously scented from her bedroom.

I felt a deliciously naughty twinge of complete abandon as I opened the door of her room, and cautiously picked through her belongings. Despite there being no place to hide a bottle in her coffin-narrow closet, I still looked there, heart thudding relentlessly in my chest as I touched and fingered each spangled costume in turn. But the closet was but a prelude to her dresser drawers; plunging my hands into a morass of filmy nylon and lace panties, demi-bras and garters, I probed deeper into the recesses of those wooden rectangles, without encountering anything other than satiny-slick fabric and richly embroidered trimmings. To the right of the dresser was a shoe rack . . . and in one lace-up boot shoved over the semi-circle of thick wire on the back row of the rack, I noticed a peculiar bulge. . . .

Once I'd pulled it out of the boot, I held the swirled glass bottle tightly in one hand, until the frosted surface felt skin-warm in my palm. There was half a bottle's worth of creamy-ivory fluid in there, which flowed with a sensual, luxuriant slowness when I tilted it. It wasn't viscid enough to cling to the interior of the bottle, so once I tired of pressing the container against my abdomen, until a bright reddish imprint lingered in my pale flesh, I hurried to the kitchenette, to find a clean jar with a secure lid. Draining the bottle over the wide mouth of the jar, I then rinsed out Elita's bottle, before filling it with a mixture of the two lubricants I'd purchased.

When tilted, the fluid moved almost as slowly as the bottle's original contents . And the color was virtually the same. . . .

After replacing the bottle, I felt tempted to use some of the balm on myself, but it seemed as if the application of the lotion was part of a greater ritual . . . one which might include the calling-forth of some unknown winged presence I was loathe to inadvertently invoke. There was simply so much about Elita I didn't understand—her culture, her job, her other friends. More than once, I'd listened in as she spoke to someone I assumed was her boss at the Club, a person whose sexuality was as mysterious to me as his or her requests, to which Elita would answer cryptically, yet with exotic familiarity:

("—so you want to stress that I'm *aswang*, *sigi*, *sigi*, but one thing—don't claim I'm a *mandurugo*, *sigi*? They're quite different, even though they're both beautiful. The *mandurugo*, she dies in every tale about her, *sigi*? You want something to call me besides *aswang*, try *danag*—she's something older, but more similar. Better yet, just say *filipina* . . . that's something the *aswang* and the *danag* have in common—")

I only understood filipina and the ubiquitous *sigi* (which was basically an "okay"-like bit of slang), but something about the context of her words spoke of things ancient, things most definitely female . . things I longed to understand, even as something about their implied antiquity ("—she dies in every tale about her—") simultaneously fascinated and frightened me. And after what I'd heard that old man say earlier in the day, about a winged presence on the fire escape, it was thrill enough for me to be able to slide the jar containing Elita's secret balm under my bed before I slept. When I dreamed, I dreamed of Elita, coated in that luminous unguent, albeit applied by my own hands . . . an Elita who slowly changed from smooth to feathery-soft under my expert touch. . . .

On the morning Elita was due back in the city, I dressed with care, trying on then discarding pair after pair of underwear—as I longed to wiggle into a pair of her froth, film, and frills panties, I knew such a trespass into her belongings would only tip her off about the lubricant—until I found a pair of silk tap pants, pale blush in color, with a tiny bow centered over my navel, and ruffled scallops of thread along the leg-openings. And the low-drooping French-seamed crotch rubbed hard against my inner lips and half-buried clit with exquisite sensuality—rough, yet tender. I did debate about what size "cookies" to slide into my Wonder Bra—too much padding made me look eager, yet only one pad per cup didn't quite augment my cleavage. . . .

Remembering that sexual arousal improves breast size, I slid my fingers past the wide-open leg of my tap pants, and began to slowly jiggle my pendulous outer labia, just wiggling the skin without touching my clit, until I felt the slow-burn flush of impending orgasm—and saw my breasts plump up just enough.

Standing before my closet-door mirror, I rose up on tip-toes, to simulate Elita's photo pose (or perhaps her flight from the fire-escape?), but my body was too Martha Stewartish to look sensual. Hooking one finger around the crotch of my panties, I pulled aside the fabric to reveal the plump cleft of close-clipped flesh . . . not quite Bettie Page, but closer to a Mayflower Madam type.

Somewhat of an improvement, but I doubted I'd please the crowd at Elita's Club . . . not if her boss saw fit to advertise her as some exotic being of what *had* to be filipino legend.

But I hoped that Elita might be able to help me out in that regard, once she discovered my harmless ruse. *If* she decided to work this evening, as I hoped against hope she would. . . .

My underwear was discreetly hidden under a loose sleeveless tee and a wrap skirt by the time I heard Elita's knock on my door; that long-nailed clawing rap against the wood was unmistakable. As I hurried to the door, the flap and wind of fabric around my bare legs was exquisitely licen-

tious, as was the tugging friction of my crotch against my
tender, already moist spots—I found myself wondering if
that's how it felt when Elita's unknown customers groped
her, slid money in her G-string. She rapped the door again
as I opened the locks one after another, and as I pulled the
door open, her right hand kept moving forward, until the
slightly curled knuckles brushed the tip of one of my
breasts.

She wasn't tanned, but seemed to glow as from within,
her wide-cheeked face flushed with a ruddy pink bloom,
while her full lips—even fuller than I remembered them—
glistened with carmine, which matched the high-gloss pol-
ish on her curled-inward nails. Odd, how they now reminded me of talons. . . . Before she said anything, she pointedly
circled my nipple with her first knuckle, then moved her
hand down the surface of my tee before resting her hand,
palm down, on my stomach.

"Is that lace I feel under your tee? Such a change from the
thick, heavy things you wore before I left."

I nodded, the angled sides of my chiseled bob brushing
both my cheeks, as Elita slipped past me into the apartment, saying over her shoulder, "I hope you didn't have
anything special planned, sigi? My manager at the Club
called me in L.A. His clientele misses me . . . they've been
clamoring for their 'Kikak'. . . but I promise, I'll make it up
to you if you did have something in mind tonight, *sigi*?"
she finished from the muffling confines of her bedroom. As
I tiptoed across the living room, past the kitchenette, and
closer to her half-opened door, I heard the sussurus of her
crinkle-cotton dress sliding down her body into a heap,
then listened for the softer, more intimate sounds of
underwear moving off taut, smooth flesh. Only when I
heard her moving the shoe rack did I shuck off my tee and

shirt, and kick off my slides, until I stood all-but-undressed outside her bedroom, and when I heard the snick of the metal cap being removed from the bottle, I breathed through my mouth, hard and deep, while slipping my forefinger into my panty-leg, and caressing the contours of my mons in anticipation.

"What the—?" Elita's voice was a mixture of shock and anguish, followed by a beat of silence, then:

"You been in my room?"

That in a tone devoid of accusation; rather, there was a hint of the inevitable in her voice—albeit underscored with an unmistakable firmness.

Something I'd unconsciously wondered about was answered by that tone—Elita definitely *needed* that lotion. For what, I wasn't sure . . . but I suspected I'd soon find out. Just as I felt that I'd soon find out a *lot* of things about Elita . . . things like the *aswang*, things the people at her Club already seemed to know, and appreciate.

I pressed against the wall, hooking one finger into the natural indentation at the top of the point where my outer labia met, and as I pulled my pussy lips up tight against my pubic bone, I whispered, "Yes . . . I have. . . ."

"Then *you* have my lotion?"

"I might. . . ." I said as if I still wasn't sure if what she sought so desperately was actually something more than mere lotion.

Elita's bare feet slapped against the floor as she came out of her room to confront me, bottle of faux lotion in hand—but I honestly can't recall if she was angry, for it was the first time I'd seen her fully, gloriously nude. Unfettered by the usual moorings of her strappy pastie-like bras, her breasts jutted out from her ribcage in perfect ovals of evenly-toned creamy toffee, surmounted by nipples which

resembled gumdrops licked smooth of sugar, set into a surrounding dark oval of taffy-smooth burnt umber. Her abs
were softly sculpted under an expanse of satiny flesh,
which arced out slightly with the dome of her belly, then
continued down to a pair of achingly taut outer labia, which
framed a narrow swath of glistening black-cherry colored
tightly clipped hair, which formed a shining elongated rec-
tangle against her warm-hued flesh. The edges of the thin
ribbon of hair were knife sharp, and obviously waxed to perfection, as were her plumper-than-before labia and legs. . . .

Noticing my pointed stare at her uncovered mons, Elita
smiled with her overly pouty lips and said, "It's the newest
thing in LA . . . they use collagen on both sets now. How
about making a deal . . . you can see how they feel, in
exchange for my lotion—"

"Only if I can feel you while applying that lotion—after
you've done *me* with it," I demurred, but I wasn't expecting
her reply:

"Believe me, I don't think you're quite . . . ready for what
the lotion will do *to* you. It's totally out of your realm—"

"I've been to places like the place you work," I coun-
tered, while defensively massaging my throbbing clit with
one circling fingertip, "and I've even had offers of employ-
ment. So I think I am ready . . . Kikak. Although I don't
think our elderly neighbor down the hall will be too thrilled
when your . . . familiar comes flapping back—"

"Someone heard?" Her large dark eyes grew rounder, the
pupils expanding to all but fill the iris.

"Your little bird friend has a loud cry, or so says our
neighbor," I hissed through the first jerking twinges of
orgasm.

"My 'little bird friend'. . . so do you . . . think that it is
something I use in my act?" Elita teased, as she came close

enough to me for the radiant heat of her bared body to pulse against my own almost-bared flesh, then ran the lacquered tip of one blunt fingernail in a lazy serpentine trail down my midriff, until she reached the elastic waistband of my panties. *Then* she hooked her finger into the band, and began to shuck the silken fabric off my barely jutting hips, letting the elastic waist scrape deliciously across my tender skin.

When her tugging finger grew close to my mons, I stopped fingering myself, and thrust my pubis outward as the slickly polished nail-tip pulled across my barely thatched mons, leaving a bright streak of hot pink-scraped flesh in its wake—not scratched bloody, but burning and tickling exquisitely just above my aching clit.

Once my panties were past the tightly cupped bulge of my buttocks, they slid down to my ankles in a puffy para-chute-like flutter of silk and trapped air, leaving me naked before Elita—save for my bra, which she deftly unhooked one-handed, before flicking it off my shoulders with those talon-like rubicund nails. Glancing down at the slight curves and low-slung twin mounds of my bare torso, I simultaneously remembered Elita's question and that club manager's tacit insinuation that I wasn't evening-show "built" and found myself murmuring, "I doubt that you need anything in your act . . . but when he said your bird made a 'kaaakak'! sound, I knew it had to be yours—"

"Oh, it is indeed mine . . . but as I said before, you're still totally out of your realm here . . . and my deal still stands," she coaxed, as she took one of my hands in hers and placed it on her firm-yet-pliant protruding labia. After only the briefest of massaging strokes, I pulled my hand away as I shook my head.

"Me first . . . because I know where your lotion is. And

unless you find it, you won't be doing any dances on any laps tonight—"

The mention of the word "laps" made her caramel features flush brightly, and her eyes glittered a little too brightly as she quickly demurred, "What I do at the club has nothing to do with lap dancing . . . it isn't anything you'd understand—anything you *could* understand—"

"Like I can't understand about things like '*aswangs*' and '*mandurugos*'—I know that what I've got hidden from you is more important than a bottle of overpriced moisturizer from Bloomingdales . . . it's something *very* special, no?"

"Has my sweet little prep-school girl been doing some studying while I've been gone?" Elita teased, her voice oddly urgent, and as I mentally cursed myself for *not* having tried to find out the meanings of those words, I bluffed, "Well . . . I do know that without your special balm, you won't be able to call forth your feathered familiar," but as I uttered those words, a smile of relief spread across her wide-cheeked face, before she replied, "So all you fixated on was my lotion . . . and me in it. But at least you did remember how to pronounce the words correctly . . do you also remember a '*danag*'?"

Nodding, I began to breathe deeply, each breath making my unfettered breasts rise and fall against the bottom of my ribcage, as Elita inched closer to me, until we were tit to tit, and belly to belly—her collagen engorged labia brushed teasingly against my close-cropped mons—and said softly as she reached behind me to cup my buttocks in her long-nailed hands, the nail-tips digging into my cheeks, "The Isneg people in my land have a legend . . . of a woman who, while toiling in the fields, saw one of her fellow laborers cut her finger. And as an act of kindness, she sucked the wound clean . . . and then kept on sucking—" here Elita gave my ass a sudden, clenching squeeze "—because she discovered that she enjoyed the taste of blood far more than the taste of the food she was harvesting. Others soon followed her lead—" letting go of my butt she let her hands slide upward, to caress the indentation of my waist, then hooked her thumbs under my breasts, before moving each one off toward my arms "—and sucking human blood replaced farming. The woman who first discovered the allure of drinking blood was the first *danag* . . . but she and her kind are not the only beings who feast—" she grasped each of my breasts in her firm fingers and began massaging them, alternately squeezing then mashing them against my ribcage, while rythmicly teasing my mons with her own fleshy, swollen labis "—for among the Tagalogs, there is the legend of the *mandurugo*, or 'Girl of Many Loves'. . . a beautiful woman whose many husbands all withered and died in turn—save for the last, who survived her stinging kiss of sucking blood, and dispatched her in a flutter of feathery wings, and broke the cycle."

I had just begun to caress Elita's breasts when she said the last part, and I stiffened under her urgent embrace while saying, "You're not saying that . . . you're a *mandur*—"

Elita's laughter tinkled like tubular rods of hollow steel hitting each other in a strong wind in my ear as she pushed me against the wall and said, "No, my darling little white-bread princess . . . the *mandurugo* is but a creature of legend. Something like your bogeyman, only based on the truth—"

The intensity of her body resting against mine brought a fine bead of sweat between my breasts and down the middle of my buttocks; I pressed myself harder against the coolness of the wall behind me as I whispered against her shoulder, "But what . . . is the truth? What kind of . . .

creature inspired the story?"

In answer, she hooked one arm around my thigh, then used her middle fingertip to tease my aching inner labia from behind as she whispered, "How 'bout a new deal. . . . I'll tell you all about the *aswang* after you show me where the lotion is—and we use it on each other?"

Pressing my thighs tightly around her hand for a moment, I merely nodded *Yes* against her shoulder and neck, before we walked as one into my bedroom. . . .

True to her word, Elita bade me to stand against one wall in my room, arms up in the you're-under-arrest position, legs spread out slightly, before she uncapped the jar and began to massage the viscid fluid onto my body with both hands, rubbing and smearing it over my waiting flesh in a thin, oddly warm layer which made my flesh tingle and redden slightly—and she even massaged her hands through my scalp, and over the closely barbered cleft of my mons, before making sure that she'd touched every bit of bared skin, down to probing my navel and the outer edges of my anus, before quickly darting out of the room to wash her hands, saying over her shoulder as she did so, "Better pick out something of mine to wear . . . you'll need it at the Club tonight—"

I was still running my hands over my emollient-covered body, wondering how the previously sticky lotion had managed to become absorbed so quickly by my skin, when Elita returned to my bedroom, and repeated, "We don't have a lot of time, so you will need to pick out something . . . go on, pick anything you like, the fancier the better. It's all right . . . tonight's Neophyte Night at the Club. Usually that means just the customers, but I'm sure my boss won't mind me bringing along some help."

I'd been hoping that we could enjoy our mutual naked-ness and massaged-and-lotioned state of being before Elita left the apartment, but her words made my heart begin to thud furiously in my chest.

" 'Neophyte'. . . I began, as Elita sighed, before holding the jar of lotion toward me and teasing, "I'll tell you all, just as soon as you massage me, and then get into an outfit . . . as I said, we don't have all night—"

I felt incredibly *light* inside as I began to rub the fluid all over Elita's exquisitely soft, supple skin; by the time I'd worked my way down to her precision-sculpted pubic hair, and began slathering her already moist and musky inner lips and clit with the glistening lotion, it was as if I weighed no more than the jar which held the remainder of that pre-cious, glittering balm. My skin felt like a warm, satiny bal-loon, stretched taut over bones of supple but hollow reeds, and my head lolled all but weightless on my unusually lim-ber neck—I felt as if I could literally float to the ceiling, and hover in roiling bliss against the tiles there.

My hands seemed hardly heavy enough to maintain pres-sure on Elita's skin; noticing my ever-more-gentle touch, she began massaging the rest of the surplus lotion on her skin all over her body, until she was completely slathered from scalp to soles, then slid off my bed and hurried to her room, noisily rooted around in her closet with a jangle of hangers and a metallic-plastic slap-slap of sequins and rhinestone settings crashing against each other, then hur-ried back to my room two spangly, scintillating costumes in hand.

"Here, slip this on *now*—" she tersely whispered, while stepping into the panties of her fuschia and turquoise be-gemmed costume, then pulling on the twin triangles-and-straps matching bra. I tried to pick up the bright sapphirine and silver bra on the bed besides me, but my fingers didn't want to work like *fingers*—the best I could manage was a fin-like fingers-together motion. . . .

With each breath, I felt lighter and more buoyant than before, as Elita kneeled down to slip the panties over my legs and tug them up my thighs and over my hips, then shoved my almost-floating arms into the armholes of the abbreviated vest-like top . . . I think I felt her shoving back-less slides onto my feet, before she pulled me up off the bed, and hurried me through the apartment and out into the hallway.

I do remember that that was empty, although I could hear the distant sounds of a too-loud television set tuned to some laugh-track style sitcom, and the counterpoint of a faraway baby crying as Elita and I hurried for the window at the end of the hall . . . and it wasn't until I'd stepped through the opening on pins-and-needles feet, my body swaying slightly, as if my center of gravity had shifted rad-ically, that I realized that my mouth, my teeth, my tongue—all had changed.

When I went to open my lips, to ask Elita what was hap-pening, it felt as if my entire face was opening and closing with hard, beak-like snaps . . . and with each opening of my changed mouth, I felt a long, tubular tongue probe the sur-rounding coolish air—

And suddenly, there on the rusty fire escape, I felt my entire body *shift*, everything moving and dropping and ris-ing and expanding at once, until I no longer felt clammy air hitting my mostly exposed flesh, but was covered with an overlapping fluttery armor of brilliant feathers. Where my clothing had gone, I could not tell; it didn't drop to the fire escape, but when I darted my head down and to the sides,

all my now bifurcate eyes could see (in two slightly dis-
jointed planes of vision) was a huge rounded, feathery body
which extended out widely on either side of my arcing
breastbone—and in my shock, I wanted to shout out What
the *hell?* but all that emerged from my beak was a shrill,
eerie *"KaaaKAK!"*

Which was quickly echoed by Elita's altered voice, just
before she bobbed her domed head of sleek feathers in the
direction of the Village and began flapping her wings, prior
to rising up in the air—

Reflexively, I began to move what should've been my
arms, and felt a *true* buoyancy, a sensation of complete
physical abandon to the elements, as my body lifted up and
over the railing of the fire escape, and out over the darken-
ing streets lit only with small bright bursts of greenish-
tinged white, like the balls of burning fire which emerge
from a lit Roman candle. . . .

Not quite knowing *why*, I followed/flapped behind Elita's
rainbow-hued feathered form, sometimes swooping low,
other times soaring high into the ever-darkening sky, and
every few minutes, she'd call to me, "Kaaa*kak* . . .
KaaaaaKAK," but with each utterance, I began to understand her avian-altered speech. . . .

And so with each swooping glide of our large feathered
bodied, Elita "spoke" to me of the *aswang* . . . that beautiful vampire maiden of her native Philippines, who—in that
land of simple thatched roofs and open-to-the-elements
dwellings—would land on the roof of her chosen victim,
then slip her elongated thin tube of a tongue down through
the open spaces in the roof, and use the spear-tip sharp
point of the tongue to piece her prey's jugular vein. Then
she'd feast upon her chosen one, sucking up their blood
through that straw-like tongue—

As I flapped furiously to keep up with her, not daring to look down or around least the sudden rush of vertigo render me helpless, I asked, But surely *you* cannot be a vampire . . . I've heard of no such killings, no drained bodies— Slowing down so that she and I flew side by side in the murky dark sky, Elita explained, But we *aswang* need not kill our prey . . . just take what blood we need for fulfillment, before the giving of it to others, my fledgling. My mother did not feast to kill, only to feed *her* young. Instead of milk, we suckled life-blood, as had our ancestors before us. Just as we passed down the secret of the balm from mother to daughter—

I let Elita flap a few feet ahead of me before asking, as we both began to coast landward, toward many brightly strobing lights along the street below, But I don't understand . . . why did you leave behind your balm? If it is so special and so secret—

Her avian laughter was a rippling liquid trill, as Elita replied, Because to carry it with me would be too great a temptation . . . there are few necks in the West Coast I would wish to pierce. Why do you think my mother has had no more children? There is little suitable sustenance there . . . especially not suited for the suckling of the young.

Just before we would've hit into one of the bright-lit signs, she soared back up in the air, and I followed, wing/arms flapping furiously, as I asked, my "voice" a shrill keening in the cooling air, But *you* have no young . . . why then do you seek out prey?

Instead of answering directly, Elita instead told me, Stay close . . . then do what I do, as we neared an open fire escape upon which a couple slept, arms intertwined, on a sheet-covered mattress. Their bare limbs criss-crossed each other, just barely hinting at the throes of ecstasy which had to have preceded their slumber, and their heads rested on each other's bared chests . . . with their necks invitingly exposed and sensuously vulnerable.

The couple's open-air bedchamber was many stories above the street, but there was still yet another unoccupied fire escape landing above theirs. . . . And once Elita and I settled down, the rusty grating providing little purchase for our claw-like feet, she unfurled her hollow tongue and—as she shoved her opened beak close to the floor of the fire escape—aimed its sharp pointed tip at the man's neck, until the flesh there parted with a barely audible squelching sound . . . followed by the low sucking sound of Elita's long, long tongue drawing up his coppery-scented essence. Beneath me, the woman's neck was equally exposed, wholly ready for the quick jab of my hungering tongue . . . but only by imagining that the woman (she of the pale bobbed hair and equally colorless smooth skin) was my Elita, lying there on that twisted sheet. And when my tongue flowed out of my mouth, a seemingly endless sensation of elongation and shivery-cool air hitting its moist length, it took some doing to make the tip hit the slumbering woman's tender neck, but once the arrow-headed tip plunged in, and I began to suck up that spicy-sweet-metallic nectar, I began to sway in place on my rusted perch, my body growing taut beneath the alien coat of feathers, as the sleeping woman's fiery essence suffused my body—

Only when I felt Elita's wing bang into my breastbone did I stop drawing up that sweet fluid, as the woman stirred uneasily beneath us.

Removing her tongue-tip from the man's thickly muscled neck, then drawing it back into her beaked mouth, Elita turned to me and said in a rush of shrill clicks, Just

feed for pleasure . . . not to empty her. I think we're both
full enough for our clients, then—with a fluttering flap-flap
of her great wide-spread wings—Elita quitted the fire
escape, and I dutifully followed . . . after glancing down at
the still sleeping, albeit fitfully, couple below us.

Envying the closeness of bared body against naked flesh
between them, I hurried after my roommate, calling after
her, Clients? You mean, at the Club? as things started to
fall into place in my still-giddy mind.

She'd said something about "Neophyte Night" back in
our apartment, and as she zoomed down toward a building
whose façade was barely lit (save for a flickering neon sign
of bruised purplish-red whose lettering was all but unread-
able thanks to so many parts of the neon tubing being dark
or barely lit), and whose entryway was notable for the lack
of people waiting to come in, so that the lone doorman was
able to instead keep close watch on the skies above, I wondered just who the "Neophytes" were in her Club—the
patrons, or the entertainment?

No other buildings on either side of the dark-bricked
block seemed to be occupied at all; broken-out windows
gaped like translucent-toothed mouths in soot-grimed,
rough-pored faces, and even the carved figures on the upper-
most story waterspouts seemed to have lost interest in the
goings-on below, for their droppings-pitted features were
blind-eyed and vacuous against the inky skies. The street
itself was devoid of cars, and instead was lined with sagging, shining bags of odd-formed black, the twist-ties glistening bright red or plastic white in the random glow of the
streetlights.

Beside me Elita swooped down for a landing, while the
doorman (dark-garbed, with an occasional shining wink of
buckles and stud-like fasteners, his fleshy mouth dark-

smeared with a burgundy-black lipstick under kohl-lined pale eyes) watched her impassively, as if he'd witnessed such a rare avian display many, many times before . . . but when I more-clumsily landed next to her, my body again feeling quite strange as it impacted with the asphalt, then began to contract and elongate back into human form, I did notice that the man's heretofore jaded demeanor took on an expression of awe and anticipation.

It was a bit startling to hear Elita's dulcet human tones once more as she brushed off her taut, lean thighs and bared midriff—which was surrounded above and below by her turquoise and fuschia costume, just as my body was once again covered by the silvery-blue outfit she'd slid onto me back in the apartment—and said, "Tell the Boss that I've brought someone with me . . . new flesh for the feasting. And tell him that she gets full pay, same as me . . . or else I walk. Got it?"

The man merely nodded, before ducking into the double leather- covered dark burgundy doors next to that sputtering neon sign whose lettering I could now easily read: CLUB SANGUIS.

Shivering slightly in my scanty costume, I turned to Elita and whispered, my voice a breathy quaver, " 'Sanguis'. . . as in blood? Do you suck them, or do they—"

But as I took a good look at her in the wan glow of the street light almost a block away, I noticed that Elita filled out her costume much more tightly than she had in our apartment . . . her sleek belly was now more prominent, as were her globe-like breasts their jutting roundness straining the thin straps of her bra almost to the snapping point. And her color was more pronounced, more ruddy . . . glancing down at my own body, I was startled to see that I, too, had a convex stomach, and that I finally had breasts which needed no Wonderbra cookie inserts to swell invitingly above the triangular wedges of my spangled top.

And when I rubbed one hand over my swelling curves, the skin was flushed warm with suffused blood . . blood which came not from my own buried marrow, but the body of that sleeping woman blocks away—

Smiling at me as the doors swung open, and the doorman motioned for us to enter the Club Sanguis, Elita said, "Now what do *you* suppose they'll do to you?"

Remembering the thrill of piercing, then sucking the neck of that bare, supine woman on the fire escape, I walked closer to Elita, and asked, "But will it hurt? They won't take too much from me—"

"Only what they pay for," she whispered, as we walked down a long, musty-smelling hallway lined with dark wainscotting below and flocked brocade-patterned wall paper above; wall sconces (electric, not gas) dotted the length of the hallway every ten feet or so until the hall took a sharp turn to the right, and we entered a vast area punctuated only by flickering small candles floating in cut-glass bowls of ruby-bright fluid . . . one candle-lit-bowl per small round table. There were many tables ringing the central stage area, which measured perhaps twenty feet or so in diameter. Silken ropes on upright brass-colored poles surrounded the stage, like a birthday cake whose candles were placed precariously close to the outer rim. Motioning for me to follow her, Elita walked past several tables occupied by people who sat silently, merely drinking her in with their dark-ringed eyes (both encircled with smudged makeup and naturally dark-fleshed below the moistly shining orbs), until she reached the stage, and bent over to wiggle through the slightly sagging silken rope barrier. The view of her spread-wide behind and the plumped-up folds of her labia, neatly bisected by the thin sting of her thong panties, made my own labia throb in anticipation, but the audience was unmoved by her display—as if anticipating something far sweeter to come.

Only when my presence became apparent to them did the audience begin to murmur; I heard (or thought I heard) some husky voice whisper "Kikak has brought us a tyro" as I wiggled through the silken restraints and tiptoed onto the stage itself. The floor was slightly springy under my high-heeled feet, but since Elita made no motion to kick off her shoes, I kept my feet likewise shod. Once the two of us were on the stage, a deep carmine glow—like the light from a bathroom heater in a fancy motel room—shone down on us from above, casting weird shadows on the surrounding audience, and bathing their flesh in a light which sucked all color from their skin, leaving only blackish lips and dark, glittering eyes suspended in their pallid faces.

There was no music playing, but Elita's body began to sway, so that her blood-engorged breasts and belly shifted seductively against her torso, as she began in a teasing whisper, "I know you've all missed me . . . your teeth have ached to sink deep into my flesh . . . your bodies have hungered for my rich blood . . . and those among you who are new to Club Sanguis, you've yet to taste me, yet to experience all of me. . . ."

And as she spoke, her voice a seductive low purr in the red-lit gloom, grunts and moans of assent greeted her words, as some of the patrons quitted their tables and began to move closer to the stage, their movements punctuated by the sound of leather rubbing against leather, or the raspy fabric-on-fabric slither of ornate, funeral-gown skirts rubbing against hose-covered legs. With each sentence, her followers came closer, until I could make out their faces . . .

human faces, but transformed with chalky powders, slathered-on matte lipsticks, and thick coats of mascara on curled lashes into the visages of the would-be undead. Hair was teased into spiky or spiral- curled imitations of gothic styles, and moving arms clanked and chimed with twists of ornate chains and antique jewelry wound around wrists or between fingers.

Some of them approached me, staring at my luxuriously supple curves and protruding breasts and soft belly with a hunger usually reserved for an object of purely sexual desire, while Elita droned on, ". . . I know you've hungered for your Kikak, just as she's longed for the sharp caress of you upon her tender flesh . . but tonight I've brought you a little surprise . . . an offering of unjaded flesh as a token of my thanks for your loyalty to me . . . for am I not your favorite? Your sanguinary temptress? Does any blood flow sweeter or hotter than mine?"

In reply, the patrons—some male, many more female— nodded in anticipation, in hungering assent, as a few of them came close enough to the silken cords which separat- ed us from the crowd, and began to reach out for Elita/Kikak, with hands dark-tipped with shining ovals of blackish lacquers.

A few of them murmured, "None flows sweeter than yours. . . . Feed us, let us suck you—"but in reply, Elita merely squeezed her breasts teasingly, and shook her well- rounded behind as she said, her voice now a harsh taunt, "Who among you is worthy of my flesh? Who shall feast upon my hidden richness?"

Suddenly, folded bills, all in high denominations, bloomed in those pale-fingered hands, and only then did Elita wiggle closer to the silken boundary of the stage, and lower herself to her knees, legs spread wide as she crouched down before a small knot of customers, and let her breasts jut through the restraining cord which separated them from her. . . . Then they were all upon her, heads bent low upon her breasts, her belly, her exposed legs, and I could hear the delicate sound of teeth rending flesh, followed by the liquid slurp and lip-puckering sucking noise of blood being taken from her body. Then I felt the rough prodding motion of something stiff and sharp-edged poking my calf, and I turned around to see a woman with slicked-back dark hair and a see-through blouse barely obscuring her own bared breasts, their nipples puckered like blackened raisins against the creamy pale surrounding globes of flesh, holding up a tightly folded $20 bill.

She smiled up at me, then motioned for me to come closer to her. Her breath was spicy, like stick cinnamon, as she whispered to me through full, dark-smeared lips, "Hunker down, like Kikak is doing. Hold on to the rope and just relax. . . . I promise, I'll be gentle with you," as she tucked the fan-folded bill into my waist-string, close to my already moist mons and labia, then began to stroke my unusually full breasts with both hands, the rounded points of her nails digging lightly into my flesh, leaving trails of flushed angry skin in their wake, before she bent her head over my left breast, and began to lick the exposed swell of flesh—then eased aside my bra-top, to expose my aching nipple, then took the wrinkled nubbin of flesh into her lips and began to suck deeply, until I felt a dribble of hot liquid flow from the tiny puckered tip. . . .

Her breath quickened against my bared breast, as her lips sucked me more urgently—and even as she nursed my wine-sweet blood, another patron shoved a folded bill into my crotch, before massaging my thighs open wider, and pulling aside my left outer labia with his or her teeth, then biting down gently, but with a piquant sudden sting of an incisor parting skin, before sucking and tonguing my dripping quim. . . .

And as one patron quitted my body, another came up to the silken rope barrier to take his or her place; my body stung pleasantly with countless nips and teasing nibbles, and with each deep suck of lips upon my flesh, I felt that other woman's blood flow out of me with the same tingling warmth which had suffused me as I'd sucked it out of *her* slumbering form. My eyes were closed against the throbbing red haze which surrounded me, but through my lowered lids, I could still see a red-veined glow, which enveloped my very being with a sensation of uninhibited lasciviousness. . . . I began to flex my breasts and belly with deep jerks of my underlying muscles, and arched my pelvis outward, toward the hungering patrons of this Club, until I no longer felt the sensation of enveloping hands or the flutter of puckered, sucking lips against my flesh.

Opening my eyes, I saw the ghosts of those hungering lips upon my body—smears and puckered circles of dark color, surrounding tiny puncture-wounds which began to close up even as I watched. Behind me, Elita's voice was lower, sated as she purred, "Does this answer all of your questions about me, my sweet?"

Shaking my head, as my eyes grew accustomed enough to the change in light to see that there were no more patrons sitting behind the floating candles in their bowls of murky red fluid, I shakily got to my feet and said, my voice unusually breathless and tiny-sounding in my ears, "Who . . . who *were* they? And how did they find you?"

As Elita walked toward me on that slightly springy stage floor, I noticed that her breasts and belly had resumed their former shape and size (although her enhanced labia still jiggled plumply on either side of her tiny panty crotch); when she was close enough to cup my now much smaller breasts in her long-nailed hands, she smiled and said, "Just people . . . who think they're vampires, or wish they were vampires. People who are quite willing to pay for the experience. When I wandered into this place, they were trying to feast on each other, with but little success. It was an awkward, almost childish club, catering to pitiful wannabes decked out in gothic finery. Their taste in clothing hasn't improved, alas, but their approach to bloodsucking has become *most* refined. When I offered myself to them, the customers were most grateful . . . and the management most intrigued. At first, I paid *them* to let me dance here . . . then they had to pay me, plus let me keep all my tips. The cover charge went up, and the attendance tripled. Word spread that a genuine vampire, an *exotic* vampire at that, was in their midst. Of course, you can imagine how business boomed after *that*—" she gave my nipples a playful tweak, before running her hands down along my waist, to my hips, then cupped my buttocks with those sharp-nailed fingers as she continued "—sometimes they're waiting outside to see my arrival . . . pity, though, that they never stick around to say good-night once the floor-show is over. I suppose they're so sated with blood that they're beyond any further titillation."

As if to illustrate her point, she pulled down my costume panties, and then knelt before me to first kiss, then probe the cleft of my mons with her now quite human tongue. I took a step or two backward, until I was leaning on the silky support rope, and after grabbing it with both hands, I spread my legs and thrust my pelvis toward Elita, who began to alternately trace the contours of my inner labia with her tongue, and nibble on those jutting wrinkled folds with her front teeth, exerting just enough pressure on that tender flesh to make my thighs quiver and my heart race in my chest—and when I came in a pulsing gush of crystal musk, I dimly became aware of the sound of someone softly clapping in the distance—

"Wha—" I began, but Elita got to her feet in a fluid motion that brought her still-shining lips up close to mine, as she whispered in my ear, "I think my Boss is quite pleased with our performance, "while a man walked into view from the furthest recesses of the Club's dark interior. He was achingly normal looking; just a man of average height and weight, thirtyish, with thinning hair that was bleached almost colorless in the Club's ruby overhead light . . . and when he spoke, his voice was equally colorless in its lack of accent:

"That was incredible, girls. . . . Who says vampires can't make it, eh? Elita, if you could convince your friend here to be a regular part of the show, I'm sure I could make it worth both your whiles. . . . Once word gets around, I might even be able to pack this place twice over each night. First the blood-suckers, then the hard-core types . . . the kind who just want a sex show, no supernatural stuff included.

"*If* you'd be willing to pull an extra shift—"

Elita looked at me, her dark eyes asking *Well?* then glanced down at her Boss, who was so much like all the other strip-joint bosses I'd spoken to that I almost wanted to laugh, even as his blasé attitude toward her true vampire nature made something inside me shiver and freeze inside, so . . . while the man waited patiently, nonchalantly, I turned to her and whispered, "Will you let me go down on you, too? At least every other night? *And* help me with the lotion each time?"

Running her hands lightly over my close-clipped mons,

her thumbs gently brushing my throbbing clit, Elita whispered, "You can suck me dry every night, as long as you'll
do *both* shows with me . . . although I suspect it will affect
your studies, no?"

Glancing down at the pile of bills which covered the
stage floor after she'd pulled away my panties, and quickly
adding them up, I said, "Oh, I think I can afford to put those
aside for a time . . . as long as your boss here makes good on
his promise to make it worth our while—" as I began to tingle anew in anticipation of Elita lavishing all of her atten-
tions on me . . . once we got her other clients out of the
way.

The voice of our boss was again disarmingly bland as he
added, "Doubling the cover charge will definitely make it
worth all our whiles—as a matter of fact, I'll drive both you
ladies home tonight, and every night, just to protect my
investment."

And as Elita and I climbed off the stage, and walked
behind the man toward the back entrance of the Club,
where his car was waiting, Elita explained, "Usually the
doorman drives me home . . . although the Boss offering to
do so isn't all that unusual—

"—all the best club owners take good care of their star
attractions," she smiled at me, while giving my right cheek
a playful squeeze.

And all during the drive home to our apartment, while
Elita and I cuddled and toyed with each other's not-quite-
sated bodies, I remembered all those strip-joint managers
I'd spoken to while trying to find out where Elita/Kikak
performed, all in the hopes of merely watching her show—
and, considering that she and I were now The Show at the
Club Sanguis, I mentally made a note to stop back at that
fourteenth club I'd visited, the one whose obviously gay

owner had made that remark about birds of a feather—

—somehow, I figured that he'd be *most* interested in learning of my new nightly plumage.

He might even be interested in becoming a regular at the Club, albeit during the *first* show of the night. . . .

Desmodus
Bryn Haniver

Blythe checked her watch—it wouldn't be long now, time to find a place to hide. She panned her flashlight side to side, revealing a low, wide passageway dropping unevenly into the earth. To her right was a pile of jagged limestone boulders, ancient debris from the low ceiling. She tucked herself behind one, back against the damp rock, facing upward toward the cave's exit. Clicking off her light left her in total darkness—any glow remaining in the sky didn't reach this far down. But she could hear them coming.

Blythe Williams was doing her thesis on bats and had been studying them for over three years, but this moment still made her tingle with excitement. Below her, from the big cave, tens of thousands of tiny mammals stirred, dropped from perches, and began flying upward through the passage. She could hear a few of the insect eaters already, the whisper-light flapping of their wings sliding past her boulder in the dark.

Soon they all came, a living river of flapping, clicking, chirping mammals. They swirled through the jumbled passageway, using echolocation to navigate the darkness. Blythe hunched behind her boulder as they poured past, the soft clicks and papery rasping of wings deafening.

"For the black bat, night, has flown," she whispered into the dark as the stream of life died down to a trickle. *Wonder if Tennyson ever ventured into a real bat cave? Doubt it.*

She clicked her light back on. Further down, in a side passage off the main cave somewhere, she would search for another, much smaller population of bats. They wouldn't be stirring yet—this species waited until the sun was only a memory. They were her bats, her passion, her thesis. Desmodus rotundus. Blood feeders. Kamalotz. Vampires.

The beam of her light caught a narrow slash, down low in the wall nearby. Scrambling toward it, she noticed it was nearly impossible to see from anywhere but her hiding spot. A stroke of luck, maybe. It was small though—unlikely to lead to the population of about 150 vampires Blythe figured lived in this remote, rugged cave. Still, there was something odd about this opening. The rock gave the illusion crude steps had been cut into it an eternity ago. She squeezed in.

Blythe was taller than average for an Englishwoman, but slim. Still, it was a close fit. She had to remove her small pack and lower it ahead of her. Her long hair, though braided tightly, caught an edge of the rough limestone, trapping her.

She struggled and her gasps echoed in the small passage, the sound scaring her enough to make her pause. This was Xib'alb'a, the Mayan Underworld, place of fear and magic. Cloistered life at a small college in South England had not prepared her for wilderness caves in Guatemala. Her professor had insisted she bring a friend with her on this research trip, but Blythe had no friends she'd consider asking. She loved mammals, especially bats, but was withdrawn and uncomfortable with her own species. When the grant for field research on the vampires had come through she'd jumped at it, solo or not.

With a long, slow exhalation she twisted and calmly pulled free of the rock, leaving a few strands of blonde hair behind. Thirty meters down, rubble from the ceiling choked off the passage. Stuffing her light into a small gap and peering through, she thought she could see the tunnel widening again. She propped the light against her pack and spent an exhausting twenty minutes moving loose rocks in the tight space.

When the gap was big enough Blythe squeezed through and dropped down into a low cavern, sighing with relief as she stood up—nearly. The uneven roof was a bit short for her, but still welcome. Across the floor, her flashlight lit up a woman's shape and Blythe yelped with surprise. Ignoring the pounding of her heart, she moved forward. The figure was carved, life-size, into a column of limestone. Rough in some areas, highly detailed in others, it was an astounding piece of art. And old—from the limestone deposits, it was Mayan or even earlier.

A shrine, she thought. She kept her light on the sculpture, for some reason avoiding shining it directly into the face. Blythe shuddered with excitement—it was a beautiful yet horrible female image. Petite, well rounded. Upside down.

A Bat Goddess. What a find. The feet blended into the low ceiling, but she could see the hint of claws the artist had formed. The forearms were far too long to be com-

pletely human and ended with an elongated single finger.
Down near her own feet the face, though beautiful, had dis-
tinct fangs. The head was crowned by the tall, leaflike ears
of the vampire bat. Blythe found herself sitting in front of
it, staring.

She spotted a small inscription and gasped—she knew little about archaeology but recognized this glyph. It was old
Mayan for kamalotz, the vampire bat, inscribed like a tattoo on the right breast. She moved her hand over the inverted chest, her fingers pressing the smooth, ancient limestone. Was it supposed to represent skin, or soft fur?

"Both," whispered a voice and Blythe lurched to her feet,
stifling a scream. Her legs betrayed her, tingling and numb,
collapsing as she spun around. She fell sideways, smashing
her head into a stalactite.

Despite her caving helmet, the impact left her stunned
and gasping. She squinted at the high opening of the cave.
A head appeared. A woman's head, ears twitching. Upside
down.

Vision blurred by tears and shock, Blythe still saw the
two triangular incisors. Chisels—for scraping, not punctur-
ing like in the legends. Things got fuzzy, then dark.

Her back was cool, her front warm. She was lying face-up
on cool limestone. She couldn't see—everything was black.
But she could feel. Something warm along her left side.
Something moving down her neck, and odd sound.
Metallic. The zipper to her fleece.

Blythe sighed as wet heat pressed against her neck,
swirling pleasantly. She stirred but couldn't sit up. She
reached out and felt soft curves that her hands began to
roam over. It was warm, like sable, like exquisite fur and

now the liquid heat moved from her neck down over her collarbone. She could feel cool air. Cool moist air—she must still be in the cave.

She felt slight tugs and knew her fleece was being opened up, exposing her naked chest. Apprehension and embarrassment were smothered by the warmth which enveloped her right nipple. She gasped and clutched at whatever was alongside her but instead of pushing, her hands swept along the sleek lines, exciting her further.

Pain, a quick scrape on her chest, and now she really fought to rise but was pinned down and something began working its way into the band of her canvas pants. A weight and warmth settled onto her as her legs parted and she was gently opened up. Something firm, a finger or smooth claw, slid into her and she could hear her own moaning now as she squirmed between the cool limestone and the moving warmth.

Blythe started gasping, not getting enough air; she could hear soft lapping noises at her chest. She strained her eyes but it was still black, no it was brown, brown like fur, like the membrane of a bat's wing. She began screaming with fear and excitement and the veil came off her eyes and she could see the cave in the glow of her forgotten flashlight, could see the tall ears and mesmerizing face of the woman at her chest, the dull glint of her own blood, the odd joint of the arm or wing moving inside her pants.

She saw all this now but couldn't fight it, could only stare into the huge dark eyes and watch as the long tongue lapped at her wounded breast, occasionally swirling around her stiff nipple and sending quivers through to the base of her skull. She watched her blood being consumed and all she could do was press her hips up to meet the finger that was sliding into her, firing jolts of increasing ecstasy through her entire lower body. Blythe the virgin, Blythe the biology nerd was being bled and fucked by a woman, a woman who wasn't even human, and all she could do was moan and shake with the power of it all, riding the sensations to her first orgasm, a cataclysm of feelings so forceful it swept her from consciousness again.

Blythe woke feeling weak and sore. The glow of her primary light was a dim yellow; it was lying in the corner of the small cave. She looked at the inverted statue in the corner and then glanced at her own clothing—her fleece was done up, as were her pants. *Christ what a nightmare*, she thought, grabbing her pack and fumbling for her backup light. She smiled to herself—so real I'd swear I just got laid. Then she noticed a dull stain oozing through the material over her chest.

"No," she whispered, digging out her secondary light. She was about to switch it on when something inside her head said . . .

"Wait. I'm not too fond of bright lights."

Blythe's head snapped upward and she found herself staring into the eyes of the Bat Goddess, suspended above her in a rift in the ceiling. The eyes held her, calmed her, kept her thumb from the ON switch.

"I needed your blood," the voice continued, "but your knowledge may be equally valuable. You study my kind. To help or harm them?"

"Neither directly." Blythe spoke out loud in English, unable to lie. "Industry and government fund my work to find a way to prevent vampire bats from spreading disease to livestock."

The woman frowned. "We are not sick." Blythe understood the voice in her head but did not recognize the language.

She spoke out loud again. "No but you, um, well they, the bats, can carry rabies and other diseases." Blythe felt a flash of apprehension and disbelief. *Oh God, I'm in for one hell of a rabies shot.*

She continued. "I guess I'm looking for a way to protect the livestock without exterminating the bats. I really, um, like bats."

The woman smiled and Blythe shivered with fear and excitement, captivated by the gleaming fangs.

"Then you shall continue your studies here. And we will share blood and information, you and I." A long forearm reached down and deftly brushed along the top of Blythe's head, affectionately straightening her hair. Blythe sighed— it was classic Desmodus grooming behavior and she was shocked at how good it felt.

The Bat Goddess smiled again. "Come into the main cave tomorrow night—I'll introduce you to my family." She dropped down, a twisting flash of brown fur and dark skin that wafted Blythe with cool air as the shape vanished up the narrow entrance to the cave.

The next evening Blythe stood waiting in a small clearing in the jungle. She watched as the whirlwhind of bats rose from a dark opening in the limestone bluff in front of her. This was how she'd originally found the cave. When the stream thinned and disappeared into the fading glow of sunset, she headed down. She preferred to work at night, with the majority of the bats out—it disturbed them less.

The weight of her monitoring equipment dug into her shoulders and she stopped to shift it, remembering how crazy she'd felt all day. Convincing herself it was all a delusion was not easy when all she had to do was examine her breast: the wound looked exactly like the familiar, scraping bite of a big vampire bat. A very big one.

And then there was the sex. She'd gone through bouts of tremendous shame and guilt but there was no denying it; she felt giddy and a bit sore. And connected. Waves of reassurance seemed to emanate from the bluff, calming her and calling her back.

Following what might have been whispers, delicious whispers, she easily found the medium-sized room that housed the vampires. Sweeping her red-filtered flashlight across the ceiling, she guessed there were between 150 and 200 of them. A medium sized colony for Desmodus. But from the look of the cave floor, it had been inhabited for a very long time. An excellent study group.

She set up her acoustic equipment and infrared lights, then sat down and watched the monitors, taking occasional notes. When a dark shape reached down from the low ceiling, above and slightly behind her, she tensed, but continued. When something began pulling at her braid, loosening the plaits of hair, scratching lightly at her scalp and neck, she sighed softly but kept her eyes on the monitors.

Which were showing some strange signals. The vampires were quitting their usual early night behaviors; they were alert and exited but not moving. Blythe gasped as a warm tongue moved against the back of her neck. Winglike arms came down her sides, catching the hem of her loose canvas pants. She lifted her hips, almost imperceptibly, and the arms moved down, baring her thighs to her knees.

Blythe kept staring forward, straining her eyes in the infrared, looking at the living ceiling of the cave in front of her. The monitors squeaked incessantly—what was going on? Her hands reached upward, feeling smooth curves and soft fur. Her eyes finally focused. The bats were all staring back at her. Watching.

Blythe pulled the shape downward, past the smiling eyes,

meeting the inverted lips with her own. As the Goddess released her grip on the ceiling Blythe reclined, hair spreading across the rock, legs opening. Still inverted, their bodies interlocked and a vein in Blythe's hip provided the nourishment. She squirmed and wrestled with pleasure, which the Goddess could take as well as give—Blythe worshipped with tongue and fingers.

Their bodies twisted together on the floor of the cave while Blythe's tongue paid tribute, reveling in the warm, salty taste. The Goddess shrieked and clicked and fed, her mouth lifting Blythe to a series of violent orgasms. Though weakening, Blythe refused to let up until the woman above her convulsed rapidly, her cries of pleasure causing all the bats to drop from their perches and fly excited circles around the cave.

Afterward, late in the night, the bats flew past them, heading out to seek their own blood. Alone in the dark, the two women whispered secrets to each other, biological and otherwise.

The next afternoon, an hour before sunset, Blythe was compiling some of the data at her campsite when someone said "Hola" and she nearly jumped out of her skin. She stood to face two men—the handsome younger one was smiling at her; his older, wiry companion wasn't.

"Buenas tardes," she said, her tone cautious. They were both Mexican but did not belong to the local Indian population—their features were Spanish. She was acutely aware of how remote this site was.

"You are the bat lady?" the young man asked in Spanish. She nodded and he continued. "I am called Ciro and this is

Alfonso, my father. We work with bats too. For the ranchers."

Blythe noted the equipment they were carrying and felt of stab of panic. "You kill bats you mean."

They both nodded. "You will show us the cave entrance," Alfonso demanded. He did not share the good cheer of his son.

"You cannot kill these bats—I'm studying them. I have the government's permission."

"You can study them as they die," Alfonso replied. "It is our job and if you don't show us where the cave is we'll just watch for them at sunset. It must be near your camp here."

Blythe looked at the younger man but he shrugged and said "The wife of the local rancher heard about you. She hates bats. And he is worried about his cows. They pay us well." He lifted up a small canister of the anticoagulant that was often used to target vampire bats. They transferred it to each other by grooming and then bled to death internally.

"See?" he said. "We won't kill all the bats. Just the bad ones. Los vampiros."

Blythe's mind was working furiously. She couldn't stop these two. She had to warn the Goddess. She'd know what to do.

"I see you won't help us," the older man said. "No matter—we will find a high spot and watch for the insect eaters. We will find the cave." He stomped off into the jungle and his son gave her one more sheepish smile and followed. Blythe waited until they were far enough away and then headed for the entrance.

"I can't," she whispered, "please." Blythe had her back to

the wall of the vampire's cavern, the Goddess in front of her, huge black eyes fixed on her own, the two single claws moving lightly across Blythe's exposed breasts, scratching trails of pleasure. The bats, agitated, began flying around the room.

"You must," the Goddess said, sliding down to her knees in front of Blythe. "You are part of this colony now, part of me. Family. Do it for us," she hissed as she pressed her lips against Blythe's groin. The heat from her breath pulsed through the thin canvas pants and Blythe whimpered softly.

One of the claws moved down from Blythe's chest, sliding across her stomach and deftly catching the zipper of Blythe's pants, pulling it down, exposing her completely.

"Do it for us and your science," the Goddess whispered, her lips moving against Blythe's folds. Waves of pleasure washed through her, the shifting patterns of swirling bats mesmerizing her.

"For science," moaned Blythe as she squirmed against the rock. Blood dribbled down from the scratches on each of her breasts, the narrow trails joining at her navel, moving downward to mat in her hair. The long, agile tongue of the Bat Goddess cleaned her thoroughly, relentlessly. Blythe's cries of pleasure echoed in the small cave and the bats didn't settle down until after she collapsed.

"What was that?" Ciro asked, his voice echoing down the long passage. Their powerful lights cut bright swaths through the dark.

"It looks like there's a side passage over there. Small, but possible. Check it out. Give me a yell if you find them."

One look down the tight passage and Ciro figured it wasn't the cave of the vampiros. But he could have sworn he heard someone whispering his name. Visions of the beautiful English girl enticed him. Perhaps she would be nicer if his father weren't right beside him, grouchy as always. He set down most of his equipment and squeezed into the opening.

It led to a small cave and Ciro congratulated his own judgment—there were no bats. But he jumped as his flashlight stopped on the girl, unmoving in a corner of the room. Where was her light? What was behind her? It looked like a statue.

"What are you doing down here?" he asked, and flashed his smile. To his amazement, she began unbuttoning her shirt. Her eyes looked funny but her white breasts glowed in the beam of his flashlight and he quickly forgot about everything else. He set his light down at a romantic angle and moved toward her. Up above, hidden in recesses of the ceiling, bats quivered and clicked.

Deeper in the main cave, Alfonso sniffed at a likely entrance and yelled back to his son. The loafer must still be in the side passage—there was no response. Muttering, he headed downward, soon finding himself in an obvious vampiro cave. Aiming his light at the ceiling, he gasped with surprise. It was covered with bats, about 200 of them, but none were moving. They always moved in the bright light. But these were all just staring. Straight at him.

The hairs on his neck rose and he took two involuntary steps back before recovering his nerve. From a deep gash in the ceiling directly above something lunged down at him, driving claws through the meat of his shoulders and then lifting him ten centimeters off the ground. He began to scream as he saw the inverted face of a woman snarling at him and then her triangular teeth tore into his throat. As one, the bats dropped from their roosts on the ceiling and flew at him, covering his twitching, suspended body, lapping at his life as it pulsed out of him. Very little of his blood found its way to the floor.

Ciro couldn't believe his luck. He was on top of the English girl, thrusting inside her, nearing completion. She hadn't even said a word but had pulled him into her with an icy need he had never encountered before. He was getting pretty close when he heard a faint scream.

"Papa?" he whispered, freezing and straining his ears. There was nothing else. The woman spoke now, reassuring him, licking his neck, clutching his ass and pulling.

Blythe sighed as she felt him begin to push again. She was doing her part—he felt good inside her and she knew she would be rewarded. His movements got faster, sliding into her cool but conveniently moist opening. As he grunted she looked up, past his rocking head, and saw the Goddess moving across the ceiling toward them. Blythe was suddenly hot and moving herself, matching Ciro's frantic rhythm, looking up expectantly.

The Goddess moved directly over top and Blythe noticed her fur was dark and matted with something. She moaned and clutched at the young man with her arms, her legs and her insides. He cried out with pleasure and the Goddess dropped down from the ceiling just as he began to come. Enveloping them both, she buried her fangs in the back of his neck, shaking with the fury of bloodlust. Blythe reached around him and hung on, grinding herself to a tremendous orgasm. Caught in a moving sandwich of flesh and soft fur Ciro was swiftly drained past consciousness, fluids pumping out of him in ecstatic bursts.

When he stopped moving, Blythe gently moved his head to the side and met the bloody kiss of her Goddess. It was warm and salty and sent new shivers running through her.

Later, her body exhausted and brain numbed, she watched as the Goddess dragged the corpses into an alcove in the far end of the main cavern. Father and son were both very light—they reminded Blythe of corn husks. Not one of the vampire bats had left the cave to feed that night.

The bodies dropped into the thick guano and the huge population of insects, centipedes, and bacteria immediately went to work. When the small bats returned near dawn, all 45,000 of them, what was left of the corpses would quickly be buried. Blythe shuddered in the cool air.

"So they never found your camp?" the investigator asked her again. Blythe was sitting at her equipment table, squinting in the bright afternoon light.

"No sir. I guess they went to a different cave. How long have they been missing?"

The man shook his head. "Too long."

Blythe shrugged and eagerly turned back to her computer. The complex patterns of clicks and squeaks on the screen were finally starting to make sense.

Tripping

Margaret L. Carter

The violet grains sparkled like crushed glass and gave off a faint clove-like aroma. Mark sifted the powder from the baggie into his palm and back again. When his hands began to shake, he set the baggie down in the circle of light cast by the desk lamp and wheeled a few feet backward. With a muttered curse, he flexed his fingers and willed them to become steady. *I should be glad it's not as severe as eight months ago*, he told himself. The experimental medication had reversed most of the numbness and weakness. He no longer got so tired he could hardly drag himself out of bed, the way he used to on some days. He hadn't succumbed to bowel or bladder incontinence yet. Lots of MS patients had it worse.

Yeah, count my blessings instead of sheep. Right! He clenched his hands into fists. *Hell, I'm only forty-six!*

Barely middle-aged, and reduced to finding his social life in the online service's "You've Got Mail" announcement. Since he'd switched to working exclusively from home, his former colleagues had never visited and seldom phoned. Just as well, after all; in his last months on the job, he'd quickly become fed up with the pitying glances and awkward silences.

So self-pity is a big improvement? Cut it out! Calming himself with a few deep breaths, he wheeled back to the desk. One of his e-mail "friends," Tim, had snail-mailed him this powdered incense from some holistic healing shop. Supposed to relieve stress, relax and invigorate the nerves. *Probably a load of New Age crap*, Mark thought. Couldn't hurt to try, though. *Might as well do it now; I can't sleep anyway.*

Mark shoved aside a stack of spreadsheets to clear space on the cherrywood desktop, then scooped a teaspoon of the violet powder into a coffee mug. He lit a match and dropped it into the cup. After a momentary flareup of blue flame, the incense settled down to smoldering, emitting a fragrance of cloves and orange blossoms. As per the directions taped to the baggie, Mark leaned close to inhale the smoke.

At once he became lightheaded, possessed by a weightless vertigo. A rainbow of light rippled before his eyes.

Whoa! The label didn't say anything about this part! An electric tingle started in his nose and radiated throughout his body. The sensation sizzled from his head downward and zapped him in the groin. For the first time in weeks, he felt a stirring there. The pressure mounted with surprising force; one MS problem he hadn't escaped was what the doctors called "ejaculatory incompetence." His right hand wandered to the front of his robe. Before he could decide whether to act on this unexpected bonus, though, he blacked out.

He stood on a flagstone path in the middle of an orchard. The same fragrance of orange blossoms and cloves hung heavy in the air. He felt euphoric but no longer dizzy. It took him a minute to register the fact that he was *standing*. Still barefoot, he wore only the terrycloth bathrobe in which he'd—fallen asleep? Passed out?

Oh, man, this is one hell of a dream! The stones felt cool under his feet; the sea-green, bell-shaped flowers on the trees looked as vivid as anything in waking life. Birdsong trilled in the background. Overhead, pale blue moths with the wingspan of pigeons flitted across a rose-colored moon in a violet sky. The time appeared to be twilight, with a couple of stars visible.

Tim's note and the label instructions had mentioned nothing like this; Mark knew he should be afraid. Instead, the euphoria persisted, with a hint of the erotic frisson he'd felt before fading into this imaginary landscape.

Exulting in the vigor of his legs, he started up the flag-stone walk. At that moment, a winged shape eclipsed the moon. Something dark swooped down and landed in front of him.

The breath caught in his throat. Hands gripped his fore-arms, hands with claws instead of nails. He froze, with a vague notion that if he held perfectly still, the creature wouldn't attack.

He stared into onyx eyes with a gleam of red at their centers. The face resembled a cat's, except that it had no whiskers, and the ears lay flat in the human position, but elongated and elfinly pointed. The creature made no hostile move. It lifted one hand to graze Mark's jawline with the claw-tip of the index finger. The brief sting, like a razor cut, sent a shock along his nerves. To his surprise, his loins tightened with momentary excitement.

"You are the first visitor I've had in a long time." It spoke in a mellow baritone with a hint of a growl. Its breath smelled like spiced wine.

It speaks English? Come on! Well, why not, since this whole place existed inside his own brain? With this reminder, he realized the monster couldn't hurt him. His fear yielded to curiosity.

With the light grip of a clawed hand, the creature led him up the walk. He glimpsed a couple of slender animals, similar to deer or gazelles but with antlers like lacy fans, gliding between the trees alongside the path. The walk rounded a curve to climb a gently sloping hillside. Black marble steps set into the turf led to the entrance of a one-story white building that reminded Mark of a Roman villa.

The creature released him, stepped back, and opened the door. "Welcome to my home. Come in, please." In speaking, it displayed a neat row of small, pointed feline teeth, the corner fangs slightly longer than the rest.

"Okay—uh, thanks." Mark scanned his host, who stood about his own height and bore a pair of bat-like wings. Its body was covered with a sleek, black pelt. Unclothed, it wore a ponderous, silver necklace with a pendant that looked like an opal except for the unlikely size of the gem, along with a pair of silver, jeweled armbands. *It? No, he.* The creature had a modestly velvet-furred penile sheath and scrotum, like a dog.

The monster led the way into the house, folding his wings to fit through the door. Mark received fleeting impressions of white walls, multicolored mosaics inlaid in the black marble floors, and archways opening on inner chambers and branching corridors. Glowing glass spheres in wall sconces provided light. The splash of water reached his ears. His host ushered him into a patio or courtyard, open to the sky, with a fountain in the center. Bushes, festooned with delicate pink flowers, perfumed the air with a gardenia-like fragrance. Wind chimes tinkled in the background.

"Sit and drink with me." His host gestured to a low couch and table. As the creature arranged himself on the cushions, Mark noticed his long, sinuous tail.

Mark sat down, with a dubious glance at the silver pitcher and goblets on the table. The liquor flowed in a golden, honeysuckle-scented stream. Holding the cup in both hands, Mark stared into the liquid depths. He recalled the warnings of myth and legend—the fate of mortals lost in fairy mounds, Persephone sampling pomegranate seeds in the kingdom of Hades. *Get hold of yourself, it's just a drug trip, remember?* He raised the goblet to his lips.

Remembering the one time he had tried mead, he braced himself for a thick, cloying brew. Instead, the drink tasted like a sweet white wine and went to his head like champagne. In the three years since the MS diagnosis, he'd cut way back on drinking, along with a lot of other activities.

Setting the cup down, he offered his hand to the creature. "Thanks. I'm Mark, by the way."

"Call me Tamiel." A velvet-furred hand closed on Mark's fingers, the claws lightly stroking his palm and wrist.

"Tamiel." The name raised echoes of familiarity. *Sounds like an angel or demon or something biblical. Well, why not? Everything here has to come from somewhere in my memory.* He took another sip of the golden wine.

"You are not afraid," said Tamiel, releasing Mark's hand

with apparent reluctance.

"No. I was—alarmed—at first, naturally. But what's to be afraid of? All this—" He waved at the fountain and the shrubbery. "This isn't real. You're a hallucination."

"Indeed?" Tamiel's mouth turned up in a fleeting smile that exposed the needle-like teeth.

"Not meaning to be rude, but I inhaled a drug and dreamed you up. Those wings are a dead giveaway, if nothing else. They'd never support a—person—of your size."

"True, according to the laws of your nature. But my nature includes certain inborn powers you would call magic." His eyes made a deliberate head-to-foot scan of Mark, who felt himself flushing in response to the examination. "So you found the gate through a drug. Interesting. All my other visitors have come by magic. You are welcome to stay as long as you wish. It's a novelty to speak to someone who has no fear of me."

"I can't stay long. Soon I'm sure to wake up." The thought gave him a pang of regret. In this dream he had his old vigor back; he could walk, and who knew what else.

"How soon?"

"No idea." Mark drained his cup and refilled it, deciding it couldn't matter whether he got sloshed here. "I've never used the stuff before. It wasn't supposed to have this effect."

"Then, if we don't know how much time we have, we had better make good use of it." Sliding closer to him on the couch, Tamiel plucked the goblet from Mark's hand and set it on the table. "I want a small repayment for my hospitality. You will not be harmed." The claw-points of his right hand encircled Mark's throat, then swept down his chest into the V of the loosely tied robe, not piercing the skin.

Mark gasped at the fiery tingle. Heat pooled in his loins. His reaction astonished him. Though he had gay friends, none had ever been more than friends. Before his condition made the question moot, he had indulged in relationships strictly with women. *But this—person—isn't just male; he's inhuman.* The two violations of taboo canceled each other out, so to speak.

So he didn't try to escape when Tamiel embraced him in silken-furred arms and began licking his neck with a rasping tongue like a cat's. At the same time, the feline tail draped over his thigh and insinuated itself between his legs. He almost pulled away in shock when the furry tip tickled his scrotum. Tamiel clasped him firmly, though, preventing a retreat. Mark's buttocks involuntarily clenched, and his balls tightened. With no conscious decision, he reached around his seducer's body to stroke the velvety fur on Tamiel's back. Mark felt muscles ripple under his palms. Meanwhile, the hot, rough tongue continued to lap at his throat. A low growl vibrated in the creature's chest. *No, not a growl. He's purring!*

Mark's head spun, the pulse pounding in his temples. His cock stiffened with nearly unbearable pressure. Uncomfortably warm, he untied his robe. His hips automatically flexed with the urge to thrust. *Good Lord, I'm being licked by a giant cat, a panther with wings—and I'm so turned on I can't see straight.*

The tongue traveled in languid swirls down his chest to his navel. The rough strokes made his skin tighten and tingle. After a probing pause, Tamiel moved still lower to circle the tip of his penis. Mark groaned aloud. Then he felt the tickle of fur on his inner thigh, followed by the nip of fangs. His brain congealed with an instant of fear. *Good grief, he's biting me!* But his body didn't listen; his prick twitched with eagerness. He let out a long sigh when the tongue returned to lapping his taut organ. Any second now—

He almost choked with frustration when the licking stopped. Tamiel moved upward, pushed him down on the divan, and lay on top of him. Mark felt the needle-teeth denting his skin. He shut his eyes to savor the tantalizing contact, The growl/purr rose in volume. A fleeting pain, like a hypodermic injection, gave way to a warm trickle. Through the fog of his excitement, Mark thought, *He's drinking my blood.* The brief ghost of fear vanished when his erection pressed into Tamiel's furred loins. A firm, slick shaft emerged to rub against Mark's penis. He thrust upward, harder, faster—At the climax, he felt as if his blood gushed forth, too, in answer to the creature's need.

Spiraling down from the heights, eyes still closed, he sank into the cushions beneath him. Tamiel's tongue, now slow and gentle, licked him clean.

Mark's eyes flew open. He found himself slumped in the wheelchair beside the desk. He felt so drained he could hardly lift his head, and his heart raced frenetically.

Oh, man, that was some weird trip! Glancing at the mug, he saw that the incense powder had burned to ash. Could the substance be a chemical relative of LSD?

He breathed deeply for several minutes until his heart rate settled down. As he turned to wheel over to the computer, he noticed a damp spot on the front of his robe. *So that part was real. But Tim didn't say a word about the stuff being an aphrodisiac.*

He booted up the computer, signed onto his online service, and typed an e-mail message to Tim: "Thanks for the incense. That was an incredibly realistic hallucination. You didn't mention those side effects. Not that I'm complaining. But are you sure it's legal?" After logging off, he dragged himself to bed.

The next morning, while shaving, Mark found a tiny cut just above his collarbone. Touching it with a fingertip, he recalled the sting of Tamiel's teeth and felt a phantom stirring between his legs. *So I scratched myself while I was semi-conscious. That's all.*

After breakfast he logged on and check his mail. Tim had replied: "Hallucination? What gives? I tried the stuff myself, and all I got was drowsy. You're kidding, right? Anyway, I'm glad you liked it. Make it last, because that's all they had in the shop. A new owner recently bought the place, and that package was part of the leftover old stock."

During his usual morning's work, Mark ruminated over Tim's remarks. *What do I really know about ol' buddy Tim, anyhow? Nothing but the claims he makes in his member profile.* Yet what motive would an Internet correspondent have for sending him an illegal drug and lying about it? Not profit—Tim had asked for no money and made it clear that he couldn't get any more of the hallucinogen.

Perhaps he was telling the truth, and this substance had reacted unpredictably with the new medication Mark was testing through the experimental program. Nevertheless, Mark knew he should at least take the powder to a lab for analysis, and he should consider reporting it, and Tim, to the authorities. He also knew he would do neither of these things.

What's to complain about, after all? The stuff didn't hurt me. Quite the opposite—it had given him the pleasure of walking again, or at least the illusion thereof, with no significantly bad aftereffects. Not to mention the first orgasm he'd had in over two months.

During lunch he received a phone call from Dr. Gottlieb, in charge of the clinic at UCLA. His heartbeat quickened in alarm at the sound of her voice. *Why's she calling me? My regular checkup is next week, and if they needed to change the time, a secretary would phone.*

Dr. Gottlieb's troubled tone confirmed his apprehensions. "Mr. Linton, I have potential bad news. Nothing has been settled yet, but I wanted to alert the patients in the study now, so if it does happen, you won't be blindsided by it."

"What's the trouble, Doctor?" He hardly needed to ask; only one kind of "bad news" could warrant a personal phone call.

"We're in danger of losing our grant. You know how deep some of the recent budget cuts are." After a strained silence, she cleared her throat and went on, "We're looking into alternative funding, of course. But if the government well dries up, it doesn't look good. Not for this particular series of trials, at any rate."

No more of whatever nameless wonder drug he'd been dosed with. He would deteriorate again, back to his original condition or worse. "Thanks for warning me."

"Remember, it's not certain yet," she said. "I'm flying up to Sacramento for a committee hearing in a couple of days. There's still hope."

Mark thanked her again and hung up. Though she meant well, he recognized the "hope" of renewed state funding as an illusion of the same magnitude as the drug-induced hallucination, only a lot less pleasurable.

He chewed his way through the rest of his turkey sandwich, which tasted as dry as if he'd left it unwrapped all day. Returning to the computer, he tried to put in an afternoon's work but had trouble focusing on the screen. He fared no better fiddling with the novel he had started after resigning his corporate job for home-based consulting. Anxiety and depression made his fingers fumble and his thoughts wander. More consistently than he liked, they meandered back to last night's dream. He recalled the moist heat of Tamiel's mouth on his skin more vividly than any real-life sexual encounter he had ever experienced. His denim shorts grew uncomfortably tight. He squirmed in the chair and struggled to force his mind back to the computer.

This is ridiculous! I'm getting hot and bothered over a horror-movie monster in a drug dream! Finally he gave in and switched off the machine. Picking up the baggie of incense and the empty mug, he wheeled into the bedroom, levered himself onto the bed, and stripped naked. He poured a larger dose into the mug, set it afire, and lay down on his back. *Here goes, through the gate.*

Two or three deep breaths of the smoke, and he felt himself spiraling down into the blackness. An instant later, with no transition, he stood on the walkway outside Tamiel's villa. As on the previous visit, he wore the same thing he had worn in real life—in this case, nothing. A breeze, cool but not chilly, played over his skin. A pair of the gazelle-like animals grazed in the shadow of the trees.

Overhead, the full moon glowed in the violet sky, flanked by a few stars. It seemed to be early evening again. *Is it always twilight here?* Mark walked up the steps to the door. Instead of knocking, he pushed it ajar and stepped inside. Like Beauty's father trespassing in the Beast's palace, he felt uneasy about disturbing the silence with knocks or shouts. He wandered through the halls, peering into empty chambers and wondering where Tamiel lurked.

The third door he tried led into a room lined with cabinets and furnished with armchairs. He opened several cupboards at random. Parchment rolls in scroll cases, musty books—Flipping through a few volumes, he stumbled on one in English, a travelogue on the Orient with an 1817 publication date.

Shaking his head in disbelief, Mark settled in the nearest chair with the book. *My unconscious mind sure goes to a lot of trouble filling in the details.*

A few seconds later, a voice interrupted his reading. "Welcome, Mark. I hoped you would return."

Startled, he dropped the book and gazed up to find Tamiel standing over him. The creature picked up the book and set it on a circular table nearby, then took a seat in the nearest chair. He reached over to clasp Mark's hand. "Solitude becomes monotonous after a while."

The claws grazed Mark's palm, then withdrew as Tamiel released his hand and leaned back. The tantalizing tickle sent a shiver up Mark's arms. To his embarrassment, his cock instantly sprang to attention. He blushed, but Tamiel took no overt notice. He only said, "I feared you might have second thoughts, after I used you to feed my appetite."

That reminder didn't do a thing to control Mark's arousal. He forced himself to answer in a level tone, "It didn't hurt a bit. But I wonder what you use for food in between visitors."

"My herd," Tamiel said. It took a minute for Mark to realize he meant the animals grazing in the orchard. "I sip from a few of the beasts every night, but they aren't completely satisfying. I grow very thirsty without the occasional taste of human blood."

"Night?" Mark seized on the neutral topic. "I thought maybe it was always dusk here."

"No, the twilight changes to dark in a regular rhythm. And for a few hours at midday, it yields to sunlight, when I sleep. The sun of this place, though, is no fierce, burning orb like yours."

"How do you know about my world? Oh, of course—the books."

Tamiel apparently noticed the skeptical amusement on his face. "You still think none of this really exists, don't you?"

"Well, if you were in my situation, you wouldn't believe it either. Look, I have a condition—a sickness. I can't walk. I won't get well; I can only get worse. And I'll probably die prematurely. Somebody gave me a package of incense—" He described the powder and its effects. "So I'm imagining all this. Not that I don't enjoy it." Again he felt himself blush.

"No doubt your disbelief kept you from fearing me at first," Tamiel said. "For that I am grateful. My other visitors have come here by accident, through misuse of magical formulae, and they were either terrified or violent, or both. After enjoying them, I sent them away, and none ever returned." He stepped over to a cabinet and took out goblets and a jug, which he uncorked to fill the cups with the same golden wine he had served before.

Mark accepted a cup and took a sip. "But where is here, anyway? In your viewpoint, I mean? I still have my doubts."

Tamiel pulled his chair closer, touched his lips to his own goblet, and set it down. "A dimensional pocket created for my exclusive use. I dwell here alone except for the lower animals that share my orchard."

Mark shook his head. "Still sounds like a fairy tale. Why are you alone?"

"That, I do not know. I have no memory of my original home or how I got here. I remember only that I committed some crime for which I was exiled to this prison, with my past blotted out."

Mark glanced around the room. "Not bad, as prisons go."

"No, I have my amusements. Books, for instance, and this." He fetched a green glass bowl from a shelf. "Look." As he leaned over, his breath ruffled Mark's hair, making the muscles of his neck and shoulder tighten. Gazing into the bowl, he saw, not the emptiness he'd expected, but a pool of swirling mist. Tamiel passed a hand over it. The mist cleared, to reveal a jungle scene, with a crocodilian beast crawling out of a stream onto the bank. At a gesture from Tamiel, the scene shifted to a snow-swept mountain, with a white, apelike primate climbing the crag.

"Incredible—it's like a crystal ball."

"A diverting toy. It can be used to view thousands of times and places. Come, show me your home." When Mark only stared at him, Tamiel said, "Gaze into the scrying vessel and concentrate."

Humoring his host, Mark thought about the bedroom of his townhouse. Once again, the mist evaporated. He saw himself lying down. His face looked thin, pinched with pain. Fumbling aside the sheet with a trembling hand, the man in the image rolled into the wheelchair, slumping as if he could barely hold his body upright. He wore a pajama shirt with no pants, and a catheter snaked out from under the shirttail.

Mark gave an involuntary cry of protest and looked away.

"Forgive me, I did not intend to distress you," Tamiel said.

"Is that—did that thing show my future?"

"One possible future out of many. Put it out of your mind." *That's right*, Mark thought. *I did this to forget, relieve stress. And other—tensions.*

After waving his hand over the bowl to erase the scene, Tamiel returned the object to its shelf. "Perhaps you would care to see the rest of my house?"

Damn, is he teasing me on purpose? He must know why I'm here! The creature's sharp-nailed fingers brushed Mark's forearm, rousing alternate chills and heat. He knew his shallow, irregular breathing must be plainly audible to those elfin ears. *I feel like a horny kid on a heavy date.*

"Tamiel, I'm not really in the mood for a tour. I'm interested in finding out more about you."

A tiny smile, revealing the mere tips of fangs. "Even though you disbelieve in my reality?"

"Your wings—may I touch them?"

"Certainly." Tamiel sat forward and flexed his wings as far as the position would allow.

Mark reached up with both hands to finger the membranes. He expected a leathery texture. Instead, they felt as delicate as parachute silk. They quivered under his caress. The creature's chest visibly rose and fell with quickened breath. Mark's hands wandered from the wings to the sleek shoulders and explored the muscular frame in leisurely spirals. Tamiel arched his back, inviting more. With one hand trailing up and down the creature's spine, Mark used the other to stroke the chest fur. A nipple hardened under his palm, and he heard the beginning of a purr. The experience felt like petting a cat, but even more sensual.

His cock throbbed with impatience. "Aren't you thirsty

now?" he blurted out.

"Oh, yes." Looking down at the rampant erection, Tamiel ran his claws around Mark's scrotum and up the shaft.

Mark shuddered. "Easy—" He gasped as Tamiel's mouth assailed his throat. The licking was even more exquisite torture than he'd remembered. He reached down to fondle his tormentor's fur-sheathed genitals. Tamiel began purring, and the tip of his prick emerged.

Mark leaned into the creature's embrace, striving for friction to relieve the ache in his groin. Instead of thrusting in response, Tamiel edged away, still tasting Mark's neck and chest. Too hard to wait any longer, Mark grasped his own cock and gave it a few vigorous strokes. The pressure surged toward release—

Tamiel gripped both his wrists and pinned his hands against the back of the chair.

"Please—I have to—" Mark squirmed and thrust, his prick twitching.

"Not yet. Your passion adds savor to your blood." The creature resumed his methodical licking.

At the same time, his tail crept into Mark's lap, swept over his balls, and twined around the root of his penis. Mark's hips rose off the chair. Tamiel's lapping increased in speed and intensity, while his tail stroked up and down. Mark moaned aloud, abandoning himself to the imminent climax. He felt nothing but ecstasy when the fangs pierced his skin. The trickle of blood felt like a hot gush equal to the spurting of his passion. The convulsions seemed to go on forever.

He collapsed in the chair, panting. After a while he felt a cloth pressed against his neck. He opened his eyes to find Tamiel standing over him. His host removed the cloth and offered him a goblet. Drinking, Mark found that it wasn't the golden wine, but a thicker, cinnamon-flavored concoction. When he tried to hand it back, Tamiel coaxed him to drink all of it.

"This potion will restore your vitality. It is important that I cause you no lasting harm."

"I don't feel harmed. I feel great." He realized that was true, for the "potion" instantly counteracted the post-orgasmic exhaustion, leaving him with only a sense of pleasant relaxation.

"If you consume this each time I taste you," said Tamiel, "you will not suffer from the small amounts of blood I take."

"Thanks." *Not that it matters, because it's imaginary blood loss.* Mark had almost forgotten that in the vividness of the experience. He set down the cup and looked around the room, intrigued that this time he hadn't blacked out and returned home immediately after consummation. *Maybe because I inhaled a bigger dose of the incense?*

"You need not go back to your own world," Tamiel said. "You can choose to remain here."

"I don't believe in 'here,' remember? Besides, I have a life back there." *For the time being, anyway.* "This isn't even my real body." He gestured toward his legs. "My real body can't walk."

"Oh, that's easily explained. Whatever magic sent you here also enabled you to shape a physical form in harmony with your ideal image of yourself. It is no less 'real' than the shell you left behind."

The word "shell" gave Mark an unpleasant shiver. He didn't like to think of his deserted body lying unconscious or even comatose on the bed at home. "Well, it's been fun, but I'd better go." He stood up.

"Take this with you." Tamiel removed one of his jeweled armbands and handed it to Mark. "It will serve as a token of my reality and a reminder that you can return whenever you wish. To visit or to stay."

Not believing for an instance that he could materialize a tangible object out of this dream, Mark fastened the ornament onto his wrist with a polite word of thanks. Tamiel escorted him to the front door. As soon as Mark stepped outside, the house and the orchard vanished into a gray fog.

He woke in bed, just as he had fallen asleep, naked—except for the armband around his wrist.

For the next few days Mark plunged into work, struggling to avoid any thought of the violet powder and the world to which it had transported him. The tiny wound on his throat might be explained away, but not the bracelet. He stuffed it into a bottom drawer and ignored it.

Of course the attempt to forget proved futile. His mind revolved ceaselessly upon Tamiel's invitation. Though Mark knew staying there would mean death here, the idea of regaining his full health and vigor allured him. And then there was the sex.

But can man live by incredible sex alone? Wouldn't I go stir-crazy, without work? Not to mention what he risked from blood loss. How long could that cinnamon-flavored potion keep him healthy? Tamiel, by his own admission, had never hosted a long-term guest. And could the—monster—be as harmless as he claimed? He had probably been exiled for good reason. *On the other hand, for however long it lasts, it'll feel great. As for work, hell, I could finish that novel.*

Laughing at himself, Mark booted up the spreadsheet

program and got back to work. As long as he could function here and now, the notion of taking a permanent vacation in Never-Never Land would remain no more than a daydream.

When he exhausted himself and had to rest, it was a different matter. He resisted the temptation to burn the incense again. Now that he knew the other world actually existed, fear crept into his perception of it. Suppose he couldn't return next time and got stuck there whether he wanted to or not? But the memory of Tamiel's sleek body and sharp kisses undermined his resolution. Lying naked in a dark bedroom each night, he couldn't help reliving every detail of those erotic encounters. His penis stirred and throbbed but never attained the firm erection he had enjoyed in the "dreams." He alternately rubbed furiously at the flaccid organ and rolled over to thrust against the mattress. This self-torture raised only a ghost of the urgency he'd experienced under the drug's influence. Once only, he managed to flog his half-erect cock into a feeble climax.

I told him I had a life here. Ha—you call this living?

Nine days after his second visit to Tamiel's realm, Dr. Gottlieb called with the news about the research grant. Funding had not been renewed. In four to six months, the study would shut down.

Mark mumbled an incoherent reply and hung up the phone. For several minutes he slumped over the desk, his face in his hands, sobbing. When he could think clearly again, he berated himself for cowardice. In support groups he'd met plenty of people with greater disabilities. *Yeah, but they've got families.* Mark had no relatives except a couple of cousins he knew only through Christmas cards. His former friends from work would feel sorry, sure, but hardly devastated over losing him. His disappearance would leave no significant hole in the universe.

So call me a coward. I don't care! I've got a way out, and I'm taking it. He dressed in shorts, T-shirt, and sandals, then crammed a few things into a backpack. No sense showing up unprepared this time. After strapping on the backpack, he sat on the side of the bed and donned the silver armband. *God help me, I'm really going to do this.*

Dumping the entire remaining baggie of incense into a cup, he lit the powder. Pungent smoke billowed up. Mark drew it deeply into his lungs. His head reeled, and the now-familiar electricity tingled through his veins and stiffened every inch of erectile tissue on his body. He closed his eyes and let the smoke waft him through the gate.

Dream-Eater

Gary Bowen

There are many breeds of vampires. Some have fangs that unsheathe like a cat's claws, some have fangs like a snake that unfold from the roof of their mouth. Some have stingers in their tongues, and some have mouths like suckers that draw your intestines out through your mouth or anus. Some are smotherers who lie heavy on your chest and crush the breath from you; some have hands as gentle as a mother to hold a baby's mouth and nose closed. Some eat blood, or semen, or organs, or shit, or life itself. I eat dreams.

I perch high above the city, roosting among the gargoyles of the cathedral. The grey slate roof is striated with subtle hues of green and purple. Moss stretches thinly across the surface of the roof, like a skin transplant that can't quite take hold over a festering burn. Bits of lead gutter scrape

loose as my claws shift and clench, shift and clench. I bring
the pieces to my mouth and lick them loose with a long
tongue, savoring the metallic sweetness of the lead. Lead is
sweet, you know. That's why children eat paint chips and
the Romans flavored their wines with it. A steady diet gives
gout-like pains in the joints, then madness.

My bones have ached for centuries. I am a dream-eater,
and there is neither death nor madness for me. I eat the poisons of men and relish them. That my body is twisted and
hunched is no indication of my mental state. I thrive on
this bizarre diet of metal and dreams. I crouch with my
brothers along the gutter, their mouths gaping to spew forth
the acid rain collected from the roof of this holy place. They
are sleek, hairless, male creatures, with leathery skin and
clawed feet and hands. They perch like birds, as if they are
about to leap into the air, but this cathedral was built in
recent memory, and the artist forgot their wings.

Yet while my kind are almost extinct, I keep my watch.
I fulfill my ancient duty, taking my rightful place upon this
house of god, for here, as ever, the demons gather. It will
not be long. This city is like any other: The cathedral was
built at the heart of the city, and then the heart died. The
rowhouses that once sheltered doctors and lawyers are now
home to adult bookstores and young men who drift along
the sidewalk, eyeing one another with lascivious thoughts.

I know their thoughts, oh yes I do. And if I am disap-
pointed in my quest for a worthy foe, then I will accept a
casual lust as my fare for the evening.

The men below me are shadows to my vision, their needs
and desires blackening them in ways they cannot imagine.
They strut, the anonymity of the meetings making them
divine, for on this night they are desirable. Any insecurities
about too old or too fat or too short or too dull are wiped

away by the god-like power of attraction. They know that all they have to do is nod and smile, and another man will be drawn to them like a worshiper to a pagan idol. They revel in it; it makes them feel invincible, even as it makes them vulnerable. Disease, murder, and despair, these are the demons that flock along with them. If I am lucky I will meet a real demon tonight, a demon with a name and history. Though it may be my undoing, yet I long for a challenge, for something other than the relentless sameness of mortal passions. And if it ends in my death, so be it. I have lived a long time and I am lonely.

A blond man paces the sidewalk, his fair hair shining like a beacon in the night. I notice him, as I have not noticed other individuals, because he is so very fair he seems to cast a light about him as he walks. His tight jeans are molded to a fit a healthy body; his denim jacket swings easily from broad shoulders. The other men stir, standing up straighter, drifting along in his wake, pretending they don't see each other, pretending they have no rivals for the attention of this newcomer.

He stops at the darkest shadow, and there is a flick of a cigarette lighter. He smokes easily, and I watch, not bothering to turn my sensitive ears his direction. I know what they say.

Then they surprise me. They walk not to the alley, or to a parked car, or a nearby walk up flat, but to the graveyard itself, shadowed over with ancient oaks, poisonous vines with beautiful white flowers climbing the wrought-iron fence. It is a private world of stone and shadow, and locked against the public. The blond man produces a bit of metal that gleams once in the street lights, then he deftly picks the lock. He quietly unwinds the chain and the gate creaks open. His dark companion, all black leather and need, slips through. He follows, then reloops the chain and hooks the padlock back in place, snapping it home. Dangerous, if his companion turns out to be a killer. But it keeps them safe from the police. Nothing is out of place here, so no one will stop and investigate.

I lift to a crouch, prehensile toes gripping the slippery roof, leaving gouges in the mossy surface as my claws find purchase. I rush to the end of the roof, wings partially unfurled against the night, cupping the air to make me lighter and less likely to slip. I am agile, but I can have accidents. Things can hurt me.

I claw my way up the gable and cling to the rooftree. An ornate iron cross decorates this end of the church, the end away from the street and the need to impress the lambs who push aside the heavy bronze doors and pass under the morose saints of the main portal. I twine myself around the cross, claws gripping slate and iron in a complex knot. My eyes rake across the graveyard, flicking across raised graves and wolfstones until I see darkness against the stone. There. They are kissing, mouths meeting while the dark one undresses the fair one, dropping his trousers to reveal pale skin and golden hair. There is no foreplay, no careful consideration of wants and needs and safety. The fair one bends over the grave, resting his elbows upon the tomb. The dark one unzips and mounts him quickly. It doesn't last long, this heaving coupling full of need but devoid of passion. And yet, it has a primal immediacy, an animal satisfaction as the brain releases all its carefully learned lessons of respect and responsibility and is freed to feel nothing but the gratification of the body. It is appealingly simple, and my own organ swells in response to it.

I hear the young man, hear his gasp and grunts and fingernails raking the stone. For a moment my vision blurs and I am high among the cliffs, the dark stone looming above the nest where my mate crouches, tail twisting coyly around her body, red eyes beaming at me from the darkness. We know nothing of men and churches and dreams, we feast only upon each other, and I spring for the embrace.

I am flying, wings spread, the graveyard coming suddenly into focus beneath me, stones rushing up at excessive speed. The two below look up, jerk apart, and the dark one runs. My wings billow and I drift across the moon, sliding down the wind to land heavily on the brick pavement before the desecrated grave. The blond man is frozen, staring at me, blue eyes wide with fear and shock.

I am intimidating. I am over six foot tall and my wingspan is tremendous. I stoop, knees bending and shoulders bowing, my wings partially drawn in. But not fully. I don't want to frighten, but I do want to overwhelm. . . .

"You gave me a dream," I hiss through pointed teeth.

He whimpers and pushes himself to his feet, hands fumbling to pull up his jeans, not bothering to tuck in his shirt. "What are you?"

"I am an eater of dreams."

"Why are you here?" The 'eating' reference makes him nervous, and he's stalling for time, one foot sliding back, trying to find the space between the headstones. I jump on top of the tomb and he shrieks in fear, turning and trying to run, but my wings enfold him. A wall of gray-black leather encloses him and he whirls to face me, face stark white with fear. His eyes dart across my face, my chest, my erection. Then he squeezes them shut.

"Please don't hurt me," he begs.

With my hand I caress his face. "No. I won't hurt you."

His eyes snap open. He is shaking in every limb. He does not gaze at me with red eyes full of lust like my mate did.

I retract my wings. "You may go."

His eyes roll left and right, trying to ascertain whether he is really free or not. Then he bolts, sneakers taking him silently across the bricks. "And don't cruise strangers!" I yell after him. A moral lesson after all. I must remember my duty. But I do not believe in it, not now, not at this moment of loneliness pierced by need. I remain squatting on the grave, bald head in my hands, wings wrapped protectively around me.

Well, then. What of the other one? The one who was so dark he was almost a demon himself? Perhaps he will have a depravity that will nourish me more fully than these casual sins.

I leap to the sky, wings driving with great thrusts to lift me high into the air. Below me the blond man startles and looks up, instinctively taking cover close by a parked truck. Yes, he is sensitive to my passing now. Will he have a phobia for bats from now on? Or will he drink too much and tell bar lies no one believes? Perhaps I should look him up and see, but not now.

I am hunting darkness.

I find my prey three blocks over, hanging outside the dark door of an unpublic gathering place. I know what's inside: heart pounding music and a great deal of beef auctioning itself to the highest bidder. The block is black with dreams and delusions, desires and fears, needs and illusions of the most ordinary sort. "Does he like me?" "Will he give me his number?" "I want to get laid!" "Oh shit, I should have used a condom." "Damn it, why is he out with that bitch?" Ordinary. But their sense of alienation magnifies their faults and make them seem truly damnable. I have seen damnation, and they are nowhere close. But that doesn't change how they feel. And those are the feelings I feast upon.

He is hanging fire in the alley, staring at the blank unmarked door, afraid to go in, afraid that if he hesitates too long someone he will know will see him standing outside a gay bar, and a leather bar at that. His mind is stuck on this fear, fear of discovery, fear of rejection. He does not think it through, does not reason, "This is a blind pig, if anyone sees me here they will think I am standing in an alley, period. If they know what is behind that door, then we are brothers in secrecy. We share the same vice."

I land behind him, dropping gently through the air to land with a soft scrabble of claws. He whirls, brown eyes starting from his head, and he squeaks, too disturbed to even scream. This time I have no mercy. I seize him, dragging him inside the wall of my wings, and clamp my mouth over his. He screams now, and I devour his scream, slurping up the dark strings of fear like spaghetti. I eat faster than he can cry, tracing the screams back to their origin, the dark, festering place in the heart that says, *I am unworthy of love.*

I burrow into the blackness, devouring the toxins of his soul, my hunger raking up the old hurts, the old betrayals, the old lies. He screams again, past history ripping loose from where it is embedded in his consciousness and vomiting into my mouth. I devour it all. I am a carrion creature, a nightbreed that feeds upon the illness and weakness of others.

He falls against me, sobbing wordlessly, our infamous kiss broken, his body limp against mine, my arms holding him up. I ease him gently to his knees. Then I cup his chin in my hand, and kneeling on one knee so that my eyes are on a level with his I speak to him.

"I have seen every horrible secret you clutch to your breast, and they are only mice, scurrying about in the darkness and gnawing holes in the walls of your mind. Do not be afraid of mice." I place one soft kiss upon his lips. "Good night. Remember, sex is a gift, not a trophy."

The alley was too narrow for me to make a good takeoff; instead I claw the bricks and run up the side of the wall on all fours, wings trailing behind me. Once I reach the roof I leap skyward.

And there is the fair one, face turned up to the sky, eyes catching me as I sail across his vision, his whole body turning to follow me. I wing gracefully away, arrowing back to my perch upon the cathedral. I easily outdistance the running patter of footsteps.

I alight and gather my wings about me, settling in the niche over the side door where once there had been a gargoyle crouched, but no more. I settled down to digest my meal, yawning sleepily. I debate quitting for the night or making another hunt. I am not entirely satisfied; the secrets I have devoured are light fare. Enough to sustain me, if need be, but not enough to satisfy me.

"Hey!" the blond man shouts up at me.

I blink at him in surprise. "How did you find me?"

"You're the only one with wings."

His observation chagrins me; my camping upon the church has passed unremarked by clergy and parishioners alike for several weeks.

"What do you want?" I glare at him, and he steps back, alarmed by the redness of my eyes.

"What did you do to that other guy?"

"I ate his nightmares."

"Huh?"

I remain silent.

He tries another conversational gambit. "Why did you let me go?"

I jump from my perch, dropping lightly to the brick path that leads to the graveyard. "Why did you come back?" I retort.

"I kept thinking about you. And I saw you a couple of times. I had no idea creatures like you existed."

I laughed hollowly. "Not many," I said. "Our prey has become too dangerous."

"What do you mean?"

"Men," I said simply. "They are not as violent as they used to be, but they are more deadly. A knife wound I can survive but not a bullet."

I stretch my wings beside me, rolling my shoulders to loosen the cramps in my back. My cock is elongating, and I shuffle sideways, claws scratching on the pavement. He notices my arousal, and his body tenses. "What do you want from me?"

"Dreams," I breathe.

He licks his lips. "What kind of dreams?"

I laugh like a cracked bell pealing. "Dreams of love and lust and mating for life. I have been alone a long time. It has been decades since I have seen a female of my own kind, and years since I have seen a male."

I circle slowly, my feet tracing out the ancient mating dance of my kind. I flex my hands, muscles of my chest and belly rippling for his benefit. I stretch my wings, furling them to a narrow case about my body, then flinging them wide as the sky. Faster I move, feet stamping and leaping, showing the agility and strength of my body, spreading my wings in magnificent display. I have not done it for fifty years, but the old memory is there, buried deep in the dreamless place in my mind, like Pandora's box waiting to be opened.

He turns as I circle him, watching me, eyes glazing over,

his body answering my call. Sweat springs up on his brow, and he rubs a hand across his eyes. "I never knew gargoyles were beautiful," he mumbles.

I want him to leap free of the earth, to lead me on the merry chase among clouds and rocky spires. I want the free fall of desire, the sweeping tide of winds. I want. . . .

I sigh and draw in my wings. I regard him over the ridged upper surface of my wings, leathery membranes cloaking me. He is not my species, and I am become tainted with a madness. It happens; in a world full of poisons we eventually discover our own particular weakness. Mine is loneliness.

His hand stretches out tentatively. "May I touch your wing?"

I nod mutely.

He touches it gently. "It's warm! And soft!" he exclaims.

"I am not a reptile."

His fingers caress the fold of my wing, tracing a long length from upper edge to a point near his belly. "It's like leather, but the softest, most flexible leather I've ever felt. It's like skin."

"It is skin," I shiver, because my wings are sensitive enough to commune with the breezes, while tough enough to ride the storm.

His hands stray across the surface of the wing, finding it naturally striated with webs of tougher material and pulsing with veins. He traces them, and I close my eyes and whimper. I cannot bear his gentleness. Then he bends his head and kisses my wing, and I stiffen, the wings going rigid beneath his mouth. He finds the natural grain of my skin and licks up and down, up and down, warm wet tongue sending astonishing feelings through me. My wings fall open and I step back, reach blindly for the gate. "Let us go inside." I wrench at the chain, but he slips between me and the iron, his lockpick going click-click, and then we are inside.

He catches me by surprise, arms wrapping around my torso, mouth finding mine. I wrap my arms around him, then fold my wings around both of us, bending my neck to devour his kiss. His hands on my hips pull my groin against his belly, his belt buckle giving me a momentary pain. He notices and looks down, then drops to his knees before me. My organ is small; my kind are not so well endowed as human males. He takes it easily into his mouth, and the feeling of his mouth sucking on me makes my head spin. Inside things began to slip loose, and feelings whirl through me.

Loss, pain and loss, my beloved mate gone for seventy years, the haunting silence of the roofs where once we had roosted in flocks, liking the craggy heights of cathedrals as well as our native rocks. Loss and loneliness, our dwindling numbers, the scarcity of births among our kind pronouncing our nearing extinction. I am alone, alone, alone. . . .

The blond hair brushes my gray groin. For this moment, at least, I am connected to another living, breathing, feeling creature. For this moment, I feel pleasure. For this moment the old miseries drift loose from their moorings and are swept away upon a rising tide of lust. I spread my wings and howl.

He drinks the seeds of my barren life without flinching. I shake and sag, and he supports me. I drop to my knees and embrace him. "I did not know there were dream-eaters among mankind," I say.

"Well, that's not quite how I'd express it, but I think I know what you mean. I just like to make people feel good."

I trace his features with my claw very gently, leaving a

faint white scratch where I caress him. "Be my mate."

He smiles. "I don't think there's room for both of us in your niche."

"Visit me then."

"Sure." Then with a mischievous glint in his eye, "Want my phone number?"

"Just your address."

"Seventeen Reed Street, Apartment C. It's on the top floor, and has a balcony. But knock first. I might have company."

Humans do not mate for life.

He has given me a great gift, this one. I treasure it. But I will spoil it with a jealous tantrum if I remain, because I want more. So I spread my wings and say, "I'll remember." Then I leap into the sky.

She Who Waits

Catherine Lundoff

It's another Thursday night down at the Crypt and there you are. Eyes rimmed black and face powdered white until you look like Gaiman's Death. Nothing but blood-red velvet and black lace will do for you tonight because you are the Countess of Bathory. The Bride of Dracula. The look is you and you are it because that's all there is. You want so much more. It's worse tonight.

All the little posers from the burbs who watch you walk in want to be you or have you. Some don't care which. Neither do you. Bad case of existential ennui all around. Just the sight of the crowd makes you yawn.

You skirt the dance floor on spiky black heels. The walls are humming to Nine Inch Nails and you can barely see your friends on the other side of the bar through the clouds of smoke. That's when you see her. The blonde at the dark

end of the bar in the biker-chick-from-hell outfit looks up
and meets your incredulous eyes. Long blonde hair yanked
back from a bony face with really odd blue eyes, lots of tat-
toos, some of them homemade. Definitely looking for the
Iron Hog Roadhouse down the street, you think dismis-
sively.

Then she smiles and those weird eyes take over. You're
drowning in a sea of blue. Warm salty waves lap at your clit
and you can feel your nipples harden. Suddenly it doesn't
matter that you're drooling over a chick who's in the wrong
bar on the wrong night. You're not even worthy to lick the
dragon tattoo that wraps the length of her muscular right
forearm. The impossible just came calling.

The smell of black leather overrides smoke and perfume and you realize you're standing between her legs in
front of the barstool. She keeps smiling. Her teeth are
very large, long, yellowish. One of them (not a canine) is
even tipped with gold. The view's enough to tell you that
this is what you've been waiting for. But then, you've
already guessed that. You reach out a tentative hand to
touch the exposed skin of her stomach and it's cold, cold-
er than anything breathing. Just like you knew it would
be. She's not even cute. Not that you care. You realize
that it isn't going to be like Anne Rice. The thought is
vaguely disappointing.

A callused hand reaches out and pinches your right nipple through the velvet dress. It's a casual gesture, like she's
your new girlfriend and she doesn't care who's watching.
The stubby fingers roll your nipple around into a hard
point, tearing a groan from your throat. The black lace
panties that you put on for tonight are getting soaked. A
line of moisture runs down your leg. She keeps smiling. Her
eyes never leave yours. The smell of your sex rises up

between you. She slips a hand between your legs and sticks a finger inside.

Classy, you think with the last little corner of your mind that you still call yours. You grab her black leather chaps and hold on for balance. The blood rushes to your face in embarrassed desire and your hips rock forward of their own accord, riding her finger. She pulls it out and licks it off. Almost against your will, you moan. She could take you now and she knows it. It wouldn't matter. There's no one else here but her.

Instead she rises to her booted feet and pulls you out onto the dance floor. Now Dead Can Dance is filling the room. The burb kids all mill around trying to figure out what they should be doing. The band's not real Goth, but the blonde favors the DJ in her distant booth with a small ironic smile. Pretty eclectic biker, you think fuzzily, for the seconds that her eyes don't own you.

You ride the music in a trance. When she breaks eye contact, you can see your friends trying really hard not to see you. It almost makes you laugh to know that you're fuck dancing with something who's almost everything they wish they were. You wish you were. She reaches up and runs her fingers through your dyed black hair, tugging on it to pull your head back. It makes you feel vulnerable and you savor the novelty. Especially when she starts kissing your neck, long teeth just grazing your skin.

You're about the same height so it's easy for her to slide a black leather covered leg between your lace stockings. Your soaking wet panties ride up between your pussy lips as you rub yourself against her thigh. She turns you slowly, teeth still sauntering over your exposed collarbone and shoulder. Your eyes are shut as she circles you to press against your back and nip her way along your neck. One cold hand rises from your waist to come to rest on your breast, short fingers stroking an already pebble-hard nipple. Her thigh is back between your legs and you grind your ass into her as you float away on the slow music.

Then the music's changed and the crowd around you is starting to notice things. Like the queen of the local scene practically fucking on the dance floor with someone that no one can quite remember seconds after they see her. She's got you by the hand. You're headed for the door. You see eyes slide away from the two of you as you go past. You wonder if they'll remember you. You wonder if you'll be back to find out.

This is it then.

That cold fact scares you for a moment. You glance around briefly at what you had. It wasn't much, but it was yours. You go with her anyway. It'll be worth it. You hope. The frat boy bouncer gives you a nasty grin on your way out the door. She looks at him. He stops smiling, and looks away, quickly. You think about how he looks at you and your friends and you step up to him. Close, very close, and you whisper against his beer-scented skin, "I'll be back." He shudders and doesn't meet your eyes. You smile tightly and follow her outside. Definitely worth it.

She's got her bike parked in the alley around the corner. It sits there, chrome gleaming under the lone light bulb in its metal cage. For a moment, you think you see a saddle and a flash of red eyes, but then they're gone. It's just you and her and a big Harley. You start breathing faster. She's right behind you now, pushing you up against the bike, bending you face-down over the seat. You've never done it like this before and you're shivering as you spread your legs and she slides up your tight velvet skirt, exposing your ass. There is the sound of tearing as she shreds your panties off and the light breeze cools your bare skin.

All of a sudden, you're rubbing your face on the leather of the seat, breathing it in. She runs a hand over your ass, then shoves one finger up your hole. You gasp into the black leather, writhing against it. She pushes her other hand inside you, and you arch your back, thrusting against her hands. The sound of the zipper on your dress fills the alley, echoing with your moans, as she pulls it down with her teeth. The dress slides off your shoulders as you lean your hands into the bike. The cool air hits your breasts, shrinking your already hard nipples. You lean back down to rub them on the seat, teasing them until you can barely stand the touch of the cool leather.

By now, she's got her whole fist in your pussy and three fingers up your ass. You thrust and thrust against the icy cold of her hands. Your juices are pouring down your legs under the lacy garters and pooling in your shoes. There are voices near by, leaving the club, and you wonder if they can see you. You hope they can. The first orgasm hits hard and you howl into the seat, muffling the sound.

She pulls her fingers out of your ass and slips off a glove you didn't know she had on. You shudder as a sharp nail draws its way down your back. The skin parts behind it and the warm blood runs quickly over your cool flesh. The pain makes you whimper. You feel her laugh quietly as she licks the wound, savoring your fear, your desire. She thrusts into you again with her other hand, and you come, every nerve screaming for more. This time you don't care who hears and you shriek. You want more. It has begun.

As her hand tugs out of you, she pulls you around to face her. You look up through a blur of smeared makeup and desire into those blue, blue eyes. They're almost glowing now. She knows what you want. She probably wanted the same thing once. Maybe. She shoves you back onto the seat and bends over you, one nail still barely tickling your clit. You squirm against her and she pulls on your hair to turn your face to the side. Her tongue caresses your neck and the pressure on your clit sends you over, bucking against her hand. Her teeth find your vein and begin to drink.

It isn't the way you thought it would be. You had more elegant circumstances in mind, something very eighteenth century. This is more like Sturgis. It hurts. You gasp as the finger on your clit twists, fingers sliding inside you. Her insistent mouth draws on the holes that she's punctured in your neck. You ride her hand. You ride her power. It leaves you floating away on the high.

Just before you pass out, she pulls away. You look dream-ily at her lean face and bloodstained teeth as she smiles down at you. She's almost glowing with health now; even her long face is rounding out a little, softening. You feel dizzy. She pushes you onto the pussy pad and climbs up in front of you. The bike roars into life and you speed out of the alley just as you are. Dress pushed down around your waist, breasts bare, wet crotch grinding against her leather chaps while you hold on as tight as you can. No one walk-ing on the sidewalk or passing in the surrounding cars seems to notice. You wish they would. You feel sleazy. The seat is soaking and you squirm against her on the wet leather, letting your body beg for more.

The building looks familiar as she pulls up in back of it. Dazed as you are, you realize that she's coming home with you. Good thing that your last roommate flaked out and you're living there alone now. She stops the bike and you climb off. She walks you up the back stairs with her hand holding the back of your neck. The ice of her skin wars with the heat from your clit.

You have no idea where your purse is. It had your keys in it. The two of you stand before your locked apartment door for a moment. "You're invited in," you whisper. She laughs softly. It's a dry, chuckling sound, like bones rubbing together. You start to shiver, out of control. She looks hard at the door. You can't imagine it defying her, and it doesn't. The deadbolt clicks and it opens slowly. You can almost feel Mrs. Arnold across the hall spying through her peephole.

The blonde stops you in the doorway and leans down to run her tongue over your bare breasts. You groan, clutching her long blonde hair while your nipples burn, burst into flame under the pressure of her tongue and teeth. She looks up at Mrs. Arnold's peephole and you hear a gasp, and the sound of feet thudding backward. You meet her eyes and smile, sinking back into the ocean that calls you. You're not shivering anymore.

Then, you're inside the apartment. It's clear that you blow most of your money on clothes. She doesn't stop to admire your minimal decor or your CD collection, though she smiles slightly at your poster from "The Hunger." She doesn't remind you of Catherine Deneuve. For the first time, you wish that she would tell you what she was like before, how she became what she is. But it's too late. You try anyway. "How did you . . . cross over?"

The blue of her eyes is starting to change, growing darker as she reaches out and casually pulls your dress down. She doesn't answer, but she grimaces speculatively, running her tongue along those long canines. You shudder a little, an involuntary reaction. She runs a hand up your thigh. You dimly remember that you still have your stockings on and you stand there shivering again while she paces slowly around you. You stifle a mental picture of tigers at the zoo. Of goats staked out at the edge of the jungle. You remember that you want this. She reaches out and lifts your chin in her hand. There is no pity in her eyes.

You reach out for what is there and fall in. Heat rushes up from your clit and you ask no more questions. She pinches your nipples hard, pushing you back onto the ratty sofa. You spread your legs as she drops between your thighs, long tongue beginning to tease your clit. All fear gone now, you ride her tongue, groaning as it tickles and coaxes you. Her fingers thrust into you one by one, thrusting and pushing, until her whole hand can fit inside. You moan, spreading your legs up and onto her shoulders to make more room. She fills you, grinding up and into your pussy walls, and you are wide open. All the while her tongue circles. You come with a shout, hands involuntarily clutching her head. She turns, sinking her teeth into the vein in your inner thigh.

Each time she drinks from you, you wander a little further out. This time, you're soaring through the clouds on a moonlit night, just like you've always dreamed of doing. There's just a small pain tying you down and you try to ignore it as you sail near the full moon. The white light shines down on you and you close your eyes against it. You fly under it, the cool winds lifting your leathery wings. This, at least, is just as you dreamed it would be. The pain becomes sharper.

You come back to find that she's not ready to let you go yet. You are tied spread-eagle and face down on your bed. A rope runs around each of your wrists and under your dilapidated mattress. She is kneeling above you, naked, with a candle in her hands. Hot wax trickles onto your back, sending a river of fire that runs from your skin to your clit and you scream. She runs an ice cube over the small burns, and you jerk away from the sensation. Her knee drives into your pussy as she does it again. And again. You tug on the ropes, fully awake as you grind back against her knee. Your clit rubs her hard cold flesh. The heat and cold and the ice of her knee all push you back into your body. You hear your voice begging hoarsely for her to stop, for her to do it again, for her to take you completely.

And she does. She bends over your writhing body, sinks her teeth into the side of your throat and drinks. You feel the blood leaving your body and you twist, tensing, muscles convulsing, as you come so hard that the ropes break. You look up to see her, head tilted back in ecstasy, mouth open, howling, your blood running down her jaw over her small white breasts. Then, the clouds are back and you are soaring away, your body still coming on the bed below you. Upward you glide until the moon winks out.

When you awaken, it is some time, hours, days, weeks, later. You are alone and it is after sundown. Things have changed. That awareness fills you with a cold happiness, like a good feed. She pulled the curtains of your room shut before she went, and you mentally thank her for this kindness, as you would thank another pack member for not killing you as a cub.You reach a tentative hand up to your mouth. They're there. You almost stand to look at yourself in the mirror before you remember that there is probably no point.

You feel restless, filled with a driving hunger. It's feeding time. You try to concentrate on being elegant, coldly sophisticated. But it's hard to feel much of anything around the need to hunt, so you rise sinuously and pace over to the closet. A black vintage dress comes to hand and you pull on your costume for the night. You go out, heading for a new bar, because that is something you understand.

It's a seedy place, the kind that the old you would have been terrified to stay in. Before the change that is running through your veins tonight, filling them, glowing, burning everything in its wake. You watch the pimps and the hustlers and the whores dispassionately, pushing their notice away when it becomes too focused. You're waiting for the right one to arrive while the scent of warm blood fills your nostrils. It's almost too much and you begin to dream as you sit at the bar, dreaming about bathing in blood, feeding until you are sated.

The big man who walks in then has dreams, too. They're unpleasant by most mortals' standards. You can read them by simply looking deep into his eyes. They're a meal in themselves. You reach out.

He's at your side in moments, cautious, but unable to say no. He's another kind of predator, but not tonight. The fight whets your appetite as he struggles first to turn away, then to imagine that the coming night will fulfill his fantasies. You pretend to sip your drink, sparely, elegantly, deflecting the interest of the bartender and the crowd at the bar.

Just for fun, you run a casual hand over the man's crotch. His arousal is sweet and you smile at him, watching his eyes widen a little in fear, his tight jeans bulging at your touch. You leave together. No one will remember you. You draw his dreams of power and pain out of him with his life's blood and leave him in an alley some blocks from the bar.

Your veins burn until you want to howl your success at the moon. Survival dictates that you do not call attention to what you are and what you have done. Not until you're better at it, at least. You note the lack of sophistication in this thought, but it doesn't bother you now. You are living dead. Child of the night.

As you walk past the Crypt on your way home, you notice that they have a flyer up for a new bouncer. It makes you laugh quietly. Perhaps you'll come back and apply for the job.

About the Authors

Gary Bowen is a gay, lefthanded writer originally from Waco, Texas. He is the author of *Diary of a Vampire* and *Man Hungry*, and the editor of *Western Trails*, all published by Masquerade Books. He has published over 200 short stories, including appearances in various "best of" anthologies, including *Best Gay Erotica: 1997*. He is a prize-winning poet, nonfiction author, and a judge for the Lambda Literary Awards. He contributes regularly to Circlet Press erotic sf/f anthologies, and his work can be found in *Wired Hard*, *Fetish Fantastic*, *SexMagick 2*, *Blood Kiss Genderflex*, and his chapbook of erotic sf/f *Queer Destinies*, among others.

Margaret L. Carter (http://members.aol.com/MLCVamp/vampcrpt.htm) has been a vampire fan since reading *Dracula* at the age of twelve, an experience that inspired her to start writing horror and fantasy. Her dissertation for a Ph.D. in English at the University of California, Irvine, included a chapter on *Dracula*. Among other writings on the supernatural in literature, she edited *Dracula: The Vampire and the Critics* (1988) and compiled *The Vampire in Literature: A Critical Bibliography* (1989). Her novels include a werewolf tale, *Shadow of the Beast* (1998), and an electronically published vampire novel, *Dark Changeling* (1999), which won the 2000 Eppie Award in horror.

Renée M. Charles's work has appeared in *Best American Erotica 1995*, *Dark Angels*, *Symphonie's Gift*, and many other erotica anthologies and magazines, including all three previous erotic vampire anthologies from Circlet Press. When not writing erotica, she tends to her multi-cat "family." She is single and has a B.S. in English.

Steve Eller lives in the North Carolina mountains with a woman, a dog, and a cat. His stories have been published in numerous magazines and anthologies. Previous Circlet Press appearances have been in *Erotica Vampirica* and *Wired Hard 2*. He is an active member of HWA.

Bryn Haniver writes from a Northwest island, juggling passions for nature, literature, and adventure travel. "Desmodus" grew from a degree in biology and far too much time alone in caves from Belize to British Columbia.

Kate Hill's fiction and poetry have appeared in several small press and online publications such as *Dreams of Decadence, The Vampire's Crypt, The Midnight Gallery, Vampire Dan's Story Emporium, The Romantic Bower, Blood Moon, Scarlet Letters, Mind Caviare,* and *genrEZONE.* Her vampire romance, *The Darkness Therein,* was released this summer by Dark Star Publications. She also publishes and co-edits the small press zine *Parchment Symbols.*

Raven Kaldera is an intersexual transgendered FTM activist, organic farmer, parent, pagan minister, and pornographer whose writings are scattered hither and yon. (Two previous vampire stories appeared in *Blood Kiss* and *Erotica Vampirica,* both from Circlet Press.) 'Tis an ill wind that blows no minds.

Catherine Lundoff lives in Minneapolis with her wonderfully supportive girlfriend and less supportive cats. Her stories have appeared in *Cherished Blood, Pillow Talk, XOddity, Lesbian Short Fiction, Electric: Best of Alyson's Lesbian Erotica,* and *Best Lesbian Erotica 1999.* She thanks the Harmony Women Writers Fund for their support while writing this story.

Mary Anne Mohanraj (http://users.lanmands.com/~mohnraj) is the author of *Torn Shapes of Desire.* She has stories in *Herotica 6, Best American Erotica 1999,* and several other anthologies. Mary Anne moderates the EROS work-shop and is editor-in-chief for the erotic webzine, *Clean Sheets* (www.cleansheets.com).

Pagan O'Leary says "After twenty itinerant years in the military, I've finally found a home in the Pacific Northwest. I play with computers and write technical materials in the daytime, and play with computers and write fiction at night. My other hobbies include leather-crafting, costuming, reading, and bellydance."

Elizabeth Thorne is a graduate student studying reproductive biology. She lives by the water in an old warehouse with windows that only face inside. This is her first publication.